Time to be loved

Kiara Hawke

Chapter One

'If I've forgotten anything, you can contact me,' Lauren called to her secretary as she grabbed her jacket from the coat-stand. Late again!

She should really try to educate herself out of this ridiculous habit of leaving at the last minute. Especially when she happened to be meeting with her most cherished client.

Mr Peter Turnbull, an astute businessman of fifty, had brought excellent profits to her equestrian centre. He owned a string of thoroughbred horses which he trained for three-day eventing, and he expected his training grounds to be as high class as his horses. She held inside her mind a great pride in knowing that she'd achieved such a task. She felt grateful, too, that he had spread the good word about her far and wide. This had resulted in important incidental business to be brought to the centre.

So why on earth had she left the meeting with him so late she wondered exasperated with herself?

'Damn! Can't you watch where you're going!' a harsh voice sliced into Lauren's senses.

'Pardon me!' she snapped back, glaring hard into the steely eyes of the stranger. She must really learn to stop rushing out of doorways only to end up accidentally bumping into people. She mentally made a note on her 'Things to learn' list. A list that became longer almost every day. 'I could say the same to you, sir.'

Best not to be too hasty in her rebuke, she thought too late, he could be a potential customer. She glanced over his clothes, and put common sense before words, for now at least. His well-cut suit was made out of the most expensive material and it looked to have been tailor-made, no cheap suit off a hanger for this gentleman. His shirt looked crisp and white, the gold tie-clip glinting in the light of the narrow corridor. She cast a glance down at his shoes. She'd learned that a man's shoes spoke much of him. Her experience told her that a well-shod man appreciated his worth and wasn't afraid to pay for the appearance. The man certainly wasn't down at heel.

'Are we just going to stand here all day?' he said with a lofty air, looking down upon her with what she saw as such open contempt that she could have socked him on the jaw. 'Or maybe I should move you out of the way?'

He cast a scathing glance over her figure, and in that moment he made her feel like it would hardly be any effort for him. He would flick her aside like a piece of fluff on his stylish suit.

'Well-dressed, but not well-mannered!' she snapped back, drawing herself up to her full height of five feet eight. She was tall for a woman, yet still managed to feel vulnerable and small beside him. It must be the shoulders, she thought. Yes, that was it. They'd padded those jacket shoulders out to offer him a more formidable appearance. Not that he needed a tailor's help. One look into those steely grey eyes would be enough for anyone. 'Manners cost nothing, you know.'

'Then why don't you try some?' he replied nonchalantly, making it more than clear he felt she wasn't enough of a challenge for him to even make the effort to rebuke her. Her hackles stirred on the back of her neck, which was a rare occurrence for her, as she could handle the most belligerent of men if the need arose. It had seemed that way until now. 'Or is the usual greeting staff here offers potential customers?'

Lauren narrowed her eyes at him whilst mentally chastising herself for wasting precious travelling minutes squabbling. He was making her later than she'd already made herself. But then all she had to do was leave. He hadn't glued her feet to the floor.

'I prefer my customers to be polite and well-mannered, sir,' she stated clearly. 'And I am beginning to wonder if you fit into such an important category. I dislike rudeness at my centre.'

Lauren had deliberately emphasised the word 'my'. She did not want to leave him in any doubt whatsoever that he was dealing with an astute and able businesswoman who could be his match any day of the week, month or year. For all the good it did her. He simply looked down upon her and smiled mockingly. 'Oh, I am aware that you're the boss lady ...'

Lauren gritted her teeth at his choice of words. Boss lady! He made her sound like some mad female tyrant driving her staff to work so hard they collapsed with the arduous exertion of it all; this was when the reverse happened to be true.

Her staff always showed respect for her consideration and acknowledgement of the effort they put into keeping up the high standard of the centre. The team worked exceptionally well, and was founded more on a family-type dynamic than a boss and employee relationship. The man didn't know what he was talking about, and she was unfortunately running out of the time needed to straighten out his facts for him.

She glanced at her watch. 'I'd like to continue our entertaining episode, sir,' she said politely, curving her lips into the sweetest smile she could manage under such rushed circumstances, and truly not meaning the sentiment behind it. She'd never felt such a sudden rush of irritation and dislike for a man. His manner prickled on her skin like speckles of red-hot cinder. 'But I'm afraid I must leave for an appointment with Peter Turnbull, you may have heard of him.'

'Yes,' he replied, a knowing glint sparkling in his eyes. 'I'm sure Peter will be waiting patiently for you ... again. I'm surprised he's tolerated your tardiness for so long. I would've have been shot of you long ago.' Lauren smiled warmly at him, determined not to let him provoke her any further. She stepped aside and swept her arm through the air. 'Please enter, sir. My secretary, Yasmin, will attend to your every whim and need.'

'Really now,' he drawled suggestively, gazing so deep into her eyes she felt he must be able to read her thoughts. 'Is this one of your sidelines?' His intent suddenly hit Lauren and she felt a warm blush sweep over her face. Good Lord, what had she said?

'No, no!' she hurriedly added, trying to mentally chase her blush away but failing completely. 'I meant ...'

'I know what you meant,' he replied coolly, lazily roaming his gaze over the fresh clear skin of her face, and warming her more. He lifted his finger and swept away a loose tendril of her shining fair hair. 'You don't offer outlets for those types of ...' He quickly smoothed the back of his finger down the soft skin of her cheek. A touch so brief, it triggered in her an instant impulse to feel it all over again. 'Needs or whims.' The fire in his touch surprised her. So great was the surprise, the pulse in her throat thundered so loudly she thought he must hear it. She could feel her chest rise and fall deeply, so that she consciously made an effort to slow it, anything to hide her unexpected reaction to his touch.

'I... I'm sorry,' she stuttered helplessly, turning from him and heading down the corridor, grateful for the cool air drifting in from the open glass doors at the entrance.

'Yasmin will tend to you!' she called back, thankful she was now on her way to meet Peter, but for an extra reason than had been present a brief five minutes ago.

Chapter Two

Lauren arrived outside and welcomed the cool air washing over her flushed flesh. She walked in brisk, graceful strides towards her car. She was tall, statuesque, pleasantly rounded in the most delectable feminine way, blessed with long flowing strawberry blonde locks that she normally wore in a tidy plait whilst at work in the centre, she had always been an eye-catcher. The turning of male heads was a common occurrence, but not one that she ever seemed to notice. She felt secure enough in herself not to need such attention.

Slipping into the driver's seat, she fastened her seatbelt and turned the ignition. Nothing happened, nothing but a short dragging sound, and then more nothing.

'Damn,' she exploded furiously, thumping her hand down on the steering wheel. Her palm smarted but she didn't care.

Why now, of all times did her battery have to go flat? Why did these annoyances always seem to happen at the most inconvenient time? Was there some sort of law of nature she didn't know about that decreed that all that could go wrong would go wrong, and do so at the most awful time? 'Now what do I do?'

She paused for a moment to think. She couldn't use her car. No point in even thinking about remedying a flat battery in the few minutes, and she had left to leave for her appointment. It would take at least an overnight charge to bring it up to being able to start her car again.

Having eliminated her car, she proceeded on to other available modes of transport she could substitute for now. Tractor … no. How would she look if she was driving up to Mr Turnbull's stables in the Perspex bubble of a tractor? Downright silly! Not quite the proper business approach, she thought sensibly. No matter how the tractor would meld into the surroundings.

Maybe she could use Yasmin's car.

Damn! Maybe not, she remembered that her secretary's car had been put into the garage for repairs that very morning, and cursed the bad timing.

'Why today of all days?' she spoke aloud, hating herself for consciously blaming Yasmin for her predicament. It had nothing to do with her. She was the best secretary she'd worked with. Punctual, well-mannered and an excellent worker for the centre, she had often waited behind to help Lauren out during busy times and emergencies. So Lauren had no right to pass any of her own blame on to her.

Lauren thought of phoning Peter as she pondered a way out of her predicament. But she decided against this course of action. No point in signalling her late arrival. He may cancel the meeting … again. This was the third time they had arranged the meeting.

due to unforeseen circumstances on both sides. She couldn't see him tolerating another postponement. The matter to be discussed had become a pressing one and she risked losing good business if it did not take place today.

Lauren glanced around herself as she puzzled a solution, her gaze soon falling upon the sleek, black BMW sitting a few feet away. She instantly guessed the owner of such expensive and showy machinery, the car showed class and wealth. Not unlike the man himself.

She couldn't ever envision such a sleek machine breaking down, and would bet her last pound that it would turn at the softest flick of the ignition key. Maybe she could ask him if he could drive her to Peter's.

What a horrible thought!

She would have to be feeling exceedingly desperate to stoop so low as to make such a request. But then wasn't that what she was … exceedingly desperate?

She could picture Peter sitting at his desk right now, keen to move on with the matters at hand. And she wasn't there!

'Oh well,' she grumbled, yanking the key out of the ignition, climbing out of the car and slamming the door closed. 'Needs must as the Devil drives!'

She wanted to punch the Devil in the jaw.

Lauren started walking briskly towards the entrance, only to find her briskness decrease into a reluctant saunter. She really didn't want to be in the least beholden to the man. She felt as though he was the type would hold it over her for decades to come, whipping it out at each and every available opportunity to embarrass the hell out of her; preferably in public or before friends and family. Those were the usual places his type liked to exercise their prowess at humiliation.

And what was she going to say to him? How to word her admission of incompetence before such a secure and mocking man, posed her a problem she was unused to dealing with.

She could count on the fingers of one hand the number of times she'd had to ask a man to come to her rescue. Living, breathing and working the centre for so many years had instilled in her the self-sufficient attitude and capability to cope with, and fix most pieces of broken down machinery. But not enough to charge a battery in five minutes flat.

Her saunter decreased to a halt. She couldn't make herself do it. She just couldn't think of any words to say to keep her from looking like an incompetent fool in his eyes.

She twisted and turned words this way and that and they still said exactly the same thing, 'I'm an idiot for not being in time for my appointment with Peter. Could I please beg you for a lift in your magnificent sleek machine whilst my own car sits there pulling chromey faces at me?'

Now stop it! She chastised herself. You're making this whole affair into something it isn't, making a range full of mountains out of a tiny molehill.

Now, just go in there and ask the man very nicely if he could assist you out of your unfortunate predicament.

She felt herself cringe at her words. She could hear his mocking laugh ring in his ears and she hadn't even reached him yet.

But she knew, just knew he was going to laugh. She'd be lucky to get out of this without at least a mocking chuckle from him.

Lauren drew in a lungful of cool air and walked into the corridor, horrified to feel the heat return to her face. She felt as though she was walking into a cauldron.

Come on, Lauren, get a grip, she pep-talked herself as she strode up the corridor.

The usual silence of the corridor that accompanied her was disturbed by the lively chatter and spurts of joyous laughter coming from her office. She fumed to herself. She guessed this was the usual response the man drew from women.

She knew Yasmin to be quite shy with strangers, and new customers to begin with, but it sounded as though her characteristic shyness had taken a walk, and been replaced by a cloying admiration for the source of her joy.

And she should be working, Lauren mused, irritated. She wasn't being paid for lazing about enjoying the company of strange men. She'd left her with a dozen letters to type out, after all. No excuse to be slacking.

Fired by her irritation at Yasmin, Lauren felt more at ease with tackling the man and asking that which needed to be asked. She walked into the office and instantly caught Yasmin's gaze with her own. A firm gaze which she'd perfected for lightly and silently chastising her employees.

It was not always appropriate to speak her discontent or disapproval to her co-workers. She preferred to wait until she could reprimand them in the kinder privacy of her office. She felt it too demeaning to her staff to do so in public. Such public reprimands often had the unwelcome effect of demoralising and alienating her staff members. A look would suffice until she summoned them into her office.

Yasmin's expression changed the instant she saw Lauren's. She had not been the receiver of the look very often but took instant notice when she did. She hurriedly set to her pc keyboard and started typing up the letters.

The man, bemused by the sudden change in Yasmin, turned to face Lauren. He smiled sardonically, 'So, you've returned.' He glanced at his watch, an expensive gold affair. Lauren glowered at King Midas as he drawled, 'I must say you make very good time for someone so tardy. There and back in what … five minutes. I am impressed.'

Smart, the man was so damn smart she wanted to sock him on his strong jaw.

'I haven't left yet.' she replied, instilling a deliberate chill in her usually soft-toned voice. She wouldn't allow him to provoke her. And she guessed it was about time he learned it wasn't one of his options. Why then were those feelings of hostility prickling every inch of her skin?

He tutted and shook his head, 'Then shouldn't you really be going? Peter will be waiting for you.'

'Thank you for stating the obvious,' she returned sharply. 'I know what a particular man he is.'

He lazily cast his glance over her once more, and Lauren felt herself curling up inside. He made her uneasy just be looking at her, as though he were seeing more than he should be seeing. She felt horribly naked.

'Not too particular it would seem,' he said coldly. His expression changed into one of distaste for what he was seeing, and Lauren felt a chill wash over her body. Every inch of her soft skin shivered with the icy glare of those steely grey eyes. She felt unnerved by him. Unable to understand why her body was reacting the way it was. Why, she felt both fire and ice.

'I have to ask you a question,' she bravely said, trying hard to push her thoughts in the proper direction but finding it difficult to do so. Her thoughts felt fragmented and she had to make some effort to draw them together enough to even think straight. What on earth was happening to her?

'My car battery has gone flat and …'

'You were wondering if I could drive you to Peters?' he graciously finished for her. He gently grasped her arm and escorted her to the door, calling a goodbye to Yasmin.

Lauren's instinct again was to draw her body away from him. She disliked the chivalry of men, as she'd managed quite well on her own so far without it.

She didn't need his kind guidance out of the office. But not just on the grounds of rejecting his chivalrous motives.

It felt as though his touch was burning through her clothes. Exciting prickles of heat tingled on her skin where his grasp lay. She felt her pulse quicken, her breathing deepen, her face flush red. She yanked her arm from him, unable to bear the heat any more. She fanned her face with her hand and sighed.

'Anything wrong?' he enquired, noticing her fanning herself.

'No!' she snapped back, annoyed at herself for being so obvious in her attempts at cooling down. 'I'm just fine. Thank you.'

He grasped her arm again and turned her to face him. He looked into her eyes, quietly roaming his gaze over her flushed skin. He shook his head, 'Hmm, I'd say you look a little fevered. Are you sure you're not coming down with anything?'

Coming down with you, she thought annoyed at herself. The man was scary. He set her nerves tingling at the slightest touch. And the only way she could see to counteract the tingling was to keep him from touching her. She determined to do just that!

She yanked her arm away again. 'I'd care for you not to touch me, please.' She stared into his eyes, returning the force in his steely orbs. 'It's not mannerly when we hardly know each other.'

He gazed deep into her azure-blue eyes and smiled darkly, 'Does that mean I can touch you more when I do know you?'

The familiar flush warmed Lauren's face again and she broke his gaze, unable to hold steady. Such wicked intent sparked in his eyes when he'd spoken his words, she felt a sweet dull aching stir, and instinctively shut it out.

'No!' she exclaimed, mustering up as much of her dwindling confidence as she was able. 'Now could we please return our attentions to the problem at hand? I'm late for my meeting.'

He stood back and swept his arm before her, 'Of course, dear lady, let us mount our trusted chariot and Godspeed!' A loud mocking laugh echoed along the corridor, biting into Lauren's senses.

She made her way out into the fresh air, wondering just how much of a punch that strong arrogant jaw would withstand. She might just try and find out one day. Her mind went back to the last arrogant man she had to deal with.

Chapter Three

Lauren was always pushed for time, running a stable and an equestrian centre was not just a full-time job, it could take up twenty-four hours a day if she let it do so. She always made a determined attempt to look fresh and well-dressed, using minimal makeup to emphasise her already attractive facial features, and made sure that her bobbed hair was always neat and well-brushed. This was not simple vanity on her part; she had a strong belief about the way she had to present herself. It was a saying these days that you shouldn't judge people by appearances, and this was probably true if you were talking about personal relationships. When it came to being a professional person dealing with clients who *did* judge you in this way she felt that this rule of thumb didn't really apply.

Personally she would have liked to run about wearing a thick jumper, jeans and riding boots, but the issue lay in that she was the public face of the business. Personally she didn't mind in the least doing any of the jobs that working with horses entailed. In the early days she not only did so to save the business, but she had dressed the way she wanted. These days, when dealing with clients, to keep the business going she had to wear, for example, a cream blouse, a flared skirt with a stylish jacket and low-heeled but still decorative shoes. This way she looked every inch the young, professional woman she was, giving off an air of being independent, successful in her own right.

She was everything she projected, but she felt life was so unfair in a lot of ways, not only did she have to maintain the professional standards of the business she had to do so while dressing and looking feminine. Anyone who said that wasn't the case was wrong, because in many ways this was still a man's world, and to maintain her place in that world she had to work about twice as hard as any man she knew.

Lauren wasn't bitter about this; she just accepted it as one of the realities of a life in which women were far from equal, despite the words enshrined in the statute books.

She was just passing through the office on the way to her meeting with Peter Turnbull when Yasmin looked up from her computer. Yasmin Blair was actually Lauren's second pair of hands without whom she could not have carried out her business, with Yasmin carrying the administrative burdens, booking hacks, dealing with potential clients, typing up documents and dealing with the tax authorities with their demands for tax returns, again because of the nature of the business.

'Anything for me?' asked Lauren, fervently hoping that there wasn't because she had to be on her way. Usually this was the case, but not today, as Yasmin raised her pretty eyebrows and waved an A5 envelope at Lauren.

'This one is in your name and marked 'urgent,' thought you'd better have a look at it.' Lauren took the envelope off her and turned it over in her hands. There was an unfamiliar watermark on it, who, she wondered, were Johnson and Porrit? But the names sent alarm bells ringing in her head. She tore the envelope open and unfolded the cream-coloured sheet within, a sickening thought of what was to come inside her head.

She was right.

'It's a letter from a firm of solicitors,' she said with barely concealed fury in her voice. Yasmin got up from her swivel chair, came over and stood beside Lauren and looked down at the letter, reading it along with her employer and friend.

'Lord Ellerslie!' the pair of them said in unison. The letter set out in legal terms the news that Lord Ellerslie had decided to sue Craigton Riding Stables for loss of land and income, contending that the Low Meadow was part of his estate. Besides a wave of fury, Lauren felt a sickening lurch inside her as she contemplated the words. As usual Yasmin was able to see the situation for what it was.

'Lauren, this is an act of desperation, can't you see that?'

'Suing someone doesn't seem to be desperate,' answered Lauren with a faint tone of despair. She shook her head, she had come through all sorts of problems that might have broken a lesser person; the deaths of her mother and more recently that of her father, so she wasn't about to give vent to despair any longer. She straightened her back and read the words over again. 'Relinquish ownership...sign over The Meadow with immediate effect...due process...Court of Session.'

'You see? They don't actually say they've made the court application,' pointed out Yasmin, 'they say that's what they're going to do. It's their way of putting the screws on you so that you make some kind of settlement.'

'Maybe I should write back and ask them to stop any action, then request the settlement we were offered before,' said Lauren, realising that she was talking out loud, venting the thoughts that had come to her when she was alone in bed at night.

Chapter Four

'Important business you're attending to?' Nathan enquired casually, interrupting her thoughts; his strong fingers gripping the leather steering wheel as he unashamedly enjoyed the feel of the expensive BMW. She watched as he barely moved the wheel to draw a response from the car as he drove through the curves and bends of the country road leading to Turnbull's rambling establishment. And all she had was a car that wouldn't budge until tomorrow at the earliest.

'Yes, I'm going to collect booking arrangements for the next few months.' she replied, thinking she had not realised just how small the BMW's interior seemed at this moment. It looked a very spacious car from the outside but felt as though it had the dimensions of a Mini on the inside, it wasn't the car, it was just simply the man's overpowering presence that made her feel this way. He exuded class and charisma and she couldn't help but be affected by it.

'Peter always trains his horses at this time of the year,' she continued, hoping that some idle chit-chat would lighten the atmosphere and concentrate her thoughts. 'There are some important competitions to be won ...'

'And lost, not everyone is lucky enough to stand on the winner's rostrum.'

Lauren nodded her head, 'I know that only too well. I entered my horse Jewel into the Burleigh Cup a few years ago but soon had to accept that neither of us would be of winning material. It wouldn't have mattered how long we'd trained. Some teams win, some lose, some learn their limitations.'

'Such wise words for one so tardy,' he said disbelievingly. 'Don't you recognise your client's limitations? Most don't enjoy having their time stretched to almost breaking point before you decide to arrive.'

Lauren bristled at his words. "No, but I'm sure they understand when unforeseen circumstances hinder my punctuality." she shot back quickly.

A loud mocking laugh rang in her ears.

'And just how many flat batteries do you have every year?' he retaliated more smartly that she cared for. 'Peter has told me that you're always arriving at the last minute. You keep him on tenterhooks all the time.'

Best place for men anyway, she thought. It was the only way to feel safe with them.

'And what right has he to speak about me with you?' she stated, annoyed at Peter for discussing her so freely with another. What happened to business confidentiality? 'I shall be having a word with him when I arrive. I don't believe I like this aspect of his business practice.'

'At least he has *some* business practice.' Nathan commented scathingly. He cast her quick glance before sweeping the BMW effortlessly round a sharp curve in the road. 'Not like a certain young lady sitting beside me.'

Yes, she was sitting beside him. Sitting so close, his masculine heat enveloped her. The tingle rippling over her skin had nothing to do with bad car design. It had everything to do with the man himself, she reluctantly acknowledged. She must drive the heat away and how better than by attacking him for being so unreasonable with her?

'Listen ...' she said, glowering at him as he mischievously cocked his head towards her. 'You hardly know me at all you're just saying what you are, based on Peter's opinion of me. I don't believe that to be a fair reference point. I think people should get to know each other first hand and make their own mind up. Not be swept away on other people's notions.'

'If I'm not mistaken, I'd say you were inviting me to dinner,' he grinned down at her.

Lauren's face flushed red. She'd never asked a man out to dinner. She had always waited until asked, as she felt sensitive to such rejection.

'I ... I'm too busy for dinner.' she mumbled breathlessly, shifting uneasily in her seat. 'And I don't ask strange men out to dine with me.'

A look of interest swept over his handsome features, 'And why would that be? I thought you were a bright, young woman who knows what she wants and goes out to get it. You certainly don't appear to be the shy type.'

Lauren felt the turn of conversation was becoming uncomfortable. He entered straight into her thoughts and spun them around without a second thought. She hadn't spoken so openly about her personal life with anyone for as long as she could remember. Maybe she avoided the topic because she'd had no personal life since she'd taken over the centre from her parents after they both passed on a few years ago. All of her energy and time had been channelled into running her business.

'So, are we going to dine with each other?' Nathan asked softly.

'I'll need to confirm Peter's bookings when I return back,' she responded. 'And then there's…'

'What is there?'

Anything! She thought. As long as it allowed her a get-out clause from the looming dinner date.

'There's … there's …'

Nathan laughed loudly.

'There's nothing to stop you coming to dinner with me,' he stated with a certainty that irritated her. He tilted his head towards her once again and drawled huskily, 'Is there?'

'No,' she replied, sighing in resignation. She crossed her arms across her ample chest and stared out of the window. 'I'll be finished for today after my meeting with Peter.'

'Then that's it all decided then,' he finished brightly, a warm smile playing on his firm lips. 'We can go out for a nice meal together and learn some more about each other. I'll pick you up at seven-thirty.'

Lauren sat still, fuming silently, unable to think of a way out. He had trapped her like a fly in a silken web and succeeded in doing so with such aplomb. She was unaccustomed to being manipulated so gently, and it grated on her with the same effect as a knife's edge being scraped along a plate. She would go to dinner with him but only because he'd left her with no other option.

It certainly wasn't because she felt drawn to knowing more about him, she lied to herself.

'Do you enjoy seafood?' he asked inquisitively, unwittingly stumbling upon one of her weaknesses.

'Yes, I do,' she replied, knowing her culinary tastes stretched to almost anything written on a menu. She'd never been a fussy eater and wasn't about to start now. 'There's a restaurant on High Street that Yasmin told me about. She told me they serve the most delicious dishes, and at competitive prices.'

'The businesswoman to the end, hmm?' he commented, nodding his head appreciatively. 'I admire a lady who is good at budgeting and recognising market pricing.'

Lauren couldn't help the twinge of warmth that his words stirred in her. At least he acknowledged that she had some business sense, even if it had been shown through a simple comment over their coming meal. She hated to admit the fact but she was starting to feel comfy with the man. He was starting to make her feel at ease with herself.

She dared to chance a glance at him. There was something in the man that set her nerves tingling. Damned if she could her finger on it, she thought, annoyed at the depth of feeling he stirred in her.

His profile looked sharp, set against the green of the passing fields. Well-coiffed raven black hair led her gaze to his gently sloping forehead, leading down to a well-shaped nose and onto a beautifully proportioned mouth. His jaw-line looked lean and strong. He wasn't carrying an ounce of extra weight, she thought enviously. She'd always managed to stay pleasantly rounded, no matter how much she'd tried to eat and exercise properly. Not that she really needed to work out as she received more than ample exercise through running her centre.

She wondered how many ladies he'd met on his travels. She couldn't envisage anything thwarting the powerful effect he had on women. She sensed his brand of electric masculinity would break down any barrier daring to stand in its way.

Nathan glanced at his wristwatch and nodded slowly. Lauren felt annoyed at his subtle reference to their timely arrival at Peter's. She determined once and for all to be rid of her tardiness.

Nathan glanced at the road-sign leading to the stables and slowed the powerful car down. 'Almost there!' he said brightly, driving through the wide gateway. 'A few minutes more.'

A few minutes too many, she thought. She needed some fresh air, and she needed even more to be out of the man's presence. Never before had a car felt so warm and suffocating.

She waited patiently as he slowed the car to a smooth halt in the stables concrete car park. Hastily, she flung the door open, jumped out and clicked the door shut behind. Waving a goodbye over her shoulder, she headed for the office entrance.

Her strides couldn't swallow the ground up quickly enough. She just wanted to disappear into Peter's office and be away from the man.

As she arrived at the entrance, she cautiously turned around to assure herself that he was preparing to leave, only to be horrified that he wasn't. He was locking his car and making a beeline for her. Men they were the bane of her life. Her thoughts flashed back to Lord Ellerslie.

Chapter Five

A few years ago, just after she had taken over the stables, she had received a message of condolence from Lord Ellerslie and a request for a meeting with him. It was an odd thing to say, but in all the years she had been in Craigton she had never met their somewhat aloof neighbour, or any of his family. Craigton District was huge and the Ellerslie estate was further up the vast hill, it was also bordered by a veritable forest of spruce, larch and Scots pine that concealed the area from the view of the stables lower down.

Lauren's family had taken over the estate when she was ten years old, inheriting it from her father's uncle, who had died intestate. The business had been run down at the time, but her father, who was a semi-professional jockey, had seen it as an opportunity to build a career, with horses, for all his family.

When her father died, not knowing much about her neighbour, Lauren returned to the business and went to visit, as if by Royal summons the neighbour she had never seen. Despite being weighed down by the burden of her recent bereavement she had taken the route to the Ellerslie estate in her new BMW, one of the fruits of her once glittering career as part of the Crown Service in Edinburgh. It was the same car she still had because she now spent little money on herself due to the needs of the stables.

There was a straight driveway about a quarter of a mile long leading to the Ellerlsie home. At first she thought she was looking at an honest-to-goodness castle. The place had turrets for goodness sake! She noticed too that it had a coat of arms with a lion and a fox displayed on a gold background, all portrayed on the flag that fluttered from one of the crenulated towers.

Looking more closely at the building she realised that the main part of the structure was that of a solid country mansion with ordinary windows and doors.

Lord Ellerslie himself was waiting at the red front door of the building. Her first impression of him was that of a tall, well-built, white haired, patrician looking gentleman at least in his late sixties. He would not have looked out of place wearing a Roman toga. His suit was of traditional, finely woven tweed. He did not wear a tie with his dark blue shirt, but she had the impression that one wasn't far off. His blue eyes sparkled as Lauren got out of her car, and she had the impression that in the past, or even now, given half the chance, he could be quite a ladies man. He shook her by the right hand. His grip was firm.

'Come in my dear.' He turned and led her through the wide hallway and straight into a huge and ornate front room with leather furnishing and various animal heads mounted on wooden plaques, on the walls including badgers, a bear, deer and a moose head complete with horns. For some reason Lauren gained the impression that Lord Ellerslie had shot some of them himself. Ellerslie bade her to sit down but remained standing for a short while.

'I would like to express my condolences over the death cf poor Edgar,' he said, referring to her father. 'He was a fine man, a good jockey, why I even backed him a few times, it's a terrible tragedy.'

The words brought her father's demise back to her, so recent was the event. Lauren took out a handkerchief and wiped away her tears.

'Still raw? Yes, well, I've had family tragedies too; my wife Mary died a few years ago, my son is dead. I can understand how you feel. What would you like to drink? Tea? Coffee?' Lauren saw that it was his way of distracting her from her sorrow.

'Tea please.' Ellerslie pulled on a cord, and a distant bell tinkled. 'The old ways are the best,' he said, sitting down opposite his guest.

A few seconds after Ellerlsie tinkled a man appeared who, from his discreet grey suit and his crisp white shirt, along with a grey tie, was the very epitome of the words 'professional servant.'

Lauren supposed that the word 'butler' was out of fashion these days but the profession positively emanated from the man.

'Chivers, fetch us tea and biscuits please,' said Ellerslie, 'and don't keep us waiting.'

'Certainly m'lord,' said Chivers, barely glancing at Lauren. She had the impression that the manservant would have been pre-warned, and that the tray would already be preloaded, just waiting for the arrival of Ellerslie's guest. This impression was reinforced a bare minute later when the manservant came back bearing a tray on which sat a pot of tea, two fine china cups and the various other accoutrements for enjoying the brew. He laid this down, and his master thanked him, then he made his exit with all the grace and discretion of the professional servant.

'Let me pour,' said Ellerslie, performing the task with consummate ease. There was an air of finality about the way he did things as if he was always used to taking control. Lauren had the impression that his dear wife Mary would have been controlled in the same way he handled all things, up to giving him an heir, until the time she slipped out of his control and into the grave with what Lauren presumed was her untimely demise.

'Now let's talk about the situation with Craigton Stables,' said Ellerlsie, 'biscuits?' Lauren refused and sipped on her excellent cup of tea as he continued. 'Quite frankly there was an issue with your father's business,' said the good Lord, directing his gaze straight into her blue eyes. 'The fact is, your father was not a well off man. However, I offered him a way of making him rich with money that he could pour into the business. We were making some way in our negotiations before his unfortunate demise. Still, I supposed he died doing what he enjoyed which most of us don't get to do.'

'The stables do need some upkeep,' said Lauren, who was still innocent of business dealings in those days. 'But I don't understand why you would try and help us.'

'The truth is, I have long had to find ways of dealing with the upkeep of this estate. To this end I made a proposal to your father that involved the Low Meadow that borders on the lower end of my land, but is technically on your fathers, sorry, yours now.' Lauren stiffened at his words. The Low Meadow was where the horses were allowed to roam free and eat grass to their hearts content besides being a place where they could exercise to their benefit without needing riders.

'I know the meadow well,' she said. 'It was a place of many happy memories; leading the horses down, sometimes six at a time, and watching them roam free as they were meant to do in nature.'

'As you will know, this area is prime building land, but due to a quirk in the boundaries it continues across the tree line and into the borders of my own estate.' He paused and sipped his tea thoughtfully. 'I hope we are both business people. Your job is to sell the services of your business, and hopefully prosper in doing so. I own a couple of farms around here and we have farm shops where we sell eggs, honey and other produce. You sell services, I sell products. Now, the other side of the coin is that I can sell you a service that turns into a product that will make us both a great deal of money.'

Chapter Six

'There's no need for you to wait,' she called to Nathan as he moved towards her. 'I can make my own way home. I'm sure Peter will offer me a lift back. Thanks for your kind thoughts though.'

Maybe if she talked sweet to him, he would slip back into his car and disappear, but then again, maybe not. She gulped dryly as she watched him stride determinedly towards her. His long muscular legs devoured the ground beneath with a taut energy that made her skin tingle. She gulped as he drew ever closer.

Oh why wasn't he listening to her?

Go back, her body was screaming, please go back. But he kept right on coming.

'Do you know I can make my own way back?' she asked breathlessly, as he arrived beside her. It took all her energy to force the heat from herself. He towered over her, just a few inches away from her trembling body. His tangy male scent was drifting into her nostrils and intensifying her trembling.

'Peter will have one of his stable-lads help to drive me back. They should be almost finished for the day so they won't drawn away from their work.'

'Lucky them,' he commented dryly, waiting for her to move aside so he could enter the office. But Lauren couldn't move even if she'd wanted to. Her feet were rooted to the spot. He tilted his head quizzically and looked at her, 'is this a habit you have, dear lady? Or is it just me who draws out this incredible talent you have for blocking doorways?'

'What?' she shook herself out of her trance, feeling a twinge of disappointment nip as she did so. She glanced back at the door. She hoped it was locked because she could easily stand there for the rest of the afternoon gazing at him. 'Oh no .. I just thought you'd heard me from the car. There's no need to drive me back.'

He smiled at her and she felt her legs weaken at the sight of his parted male lips. Such perfectly white, even teeth set against a blemish-free skin, the smallest hint of stubble owing a harsh ruggedness.

The man was absolutely gorgeous! Even she had to admit the truth to herself. Such a kissable mouth too, she thought, entranced once more, and so easily she hadn't even noticed herself drifting off.

'Hello?' his voice sounded through her hazy mist of newly-found desire. She felt his fingers gently tapping her forehead. 'Is anyone home?

To be honest, she didn't know. She felt as though her reason and common sense had decided to take the afternoon off, and all she was left with was a heady desire she could not understand for the life of her.

'Oh sorry,' she muttered dizzily. 'Did you say something?'

'Yes, about half an hour ago. I said that I have to meet Peter myself today.'

Lauren's interest piqued at his first name knowledge of her client but listened as he continued, 'We had arranged to meet in about an hour, after he'd finished his meeting with you but I'm sure he won't mind me waiting. It would be a rather silly waste of time and resources for me to leave just to return in a short while.' He smiled at her and she swore she saw a wicked glint twinkle in those eyes as he did so. 'What do you think?'

'I think you're being quite sensible,' she replied, deliberately adding sweetness to her soft voice. She didn't know what he was up to. It was too difficult to read those steely grey eyes, but she felt sure he was up to something or other.

And it was with a twinge of apprehension that she felt she may be a part of his planning.

Whatever it happened to be.

Chapter Seven

'Oh, and what would that happen to be?' asked Lauren, six years previously. On the surface she appeared to be relaxed, but she had been a trainee lawyer for a few years before this, her mind was trained to look for an argument. The whole friendly approach, the tea, the soft seat the pleasantries, these were all ways of distracting her from the fact that she was being given a hard sell. She did not often lapse into the vernacular, but she realised that he was 'sucking up to her.' at a time when she was in grief and supposedly vulnerable. She did not appreciate what he was trying to do even though to all appearances she was being pleasant and compliant.

'The truth is, Lauren, if you look at that area, which was a continuous patch of land at the bottom of Craigton hill before our ancestors even grew the trees dividing up the land, it's a tremendous opportunity. You see I have been approached by Pearhall to give them planning permission. I'm quite happy to do so, their work will connect with the town, and the money - well let's just say it will keep us both happy for a number of years.'

He let the silence hang for a while, and she knew precisely what he was doing. He had dangled the carrot of money, and he was waiting for her to ask how much, and when could she get her share? Instead Lauren put down her cup which rattled a little too much in the saucer for her liking, indicating that she was suffering from nerves, and looked him straight in the face.

'Pearhall? I know that name, let me think please.' She stretched out the silence while apparently racking her brains and saw his benign smile start to fade. She knew immediately who they were but she wanted to get the upper hand in the conversation. 'Wait, aren't they a house builder?'

'One of the best in the country,' he said. 'The area is huge, when you think about it. It would be the work of only a few days for me to arrange a meeting with them - they have an office in Glasgow, only 25 miles away, and we could both be in there and signing a contract within days. It pains me to talk money, but you could easily be talking about a million pounds for your share - or more if you negotiate.' Her eyes narrowed as he finished speaking with that note of triumph in his voice, the soft-soaping all done.

'Thank you for setting out your request,' said Lauren, noting that his smile was so broad it pushed up his skin and threatened to close the eyes that looked at her so beadily from the wrinkled folds of flesh around them. How could she have thought he was a good-looking older man? He was practically leering at her in anticipation of her favourable reply. 'You haven't really indicated the extent of their activities,' said Lauren. 'I mean, let's be blunt, they're going to build houses, aren't they?'

''Pearhall are a construction company, yes.'

'How many houses are they going to build?'

'A few, I expect.' It was at this point that Lauren had to suppress an urge to go over to the non-factual peer and swat him lightly on the jaw. She knew when she was being given the run-around, and this was it. 'Lord Ellerslie, you've been involved in this business to which you've introduced me in the last five minutes for months, possibly years, can I have a straight answer please? How many houses are they building?' It was as if she had tried to pull a tortoise out of its shell, his smile disappeared and he looked distinctly grumpy.

'The plans I have seen, well, perhaps four hundred to five hundred.'

'Private houses?'

'Well Kirkton Parish council have asked that at least 25% should be allocated as rental properties. This is a fairly rural economy, but in the main, yes.'

Lauren made a quick mental calculation. At current prices, even with the rabbit hutches they called homes these days, such dwellings would sell for a minimum of quarter a million pounds, which when you added up the potential profit for Pearhall, added up to a staggering amount of money. A million pounds for her land, in such a context, would be chicken feed.

'How many of the houses were going to be built on my land?'

'You do like your figures, don't you?' asked Ellerslie, beginning to look exasperated.

'I negotiated contracts and worked with suppliers of all kinds in my old job,' said Lauren sweetly, 'it becomes second nature.'

'Very well, if you must know, about fifty percent of the housing would be on your land, and once we get the trees cleared that could be as many as three hundred houses.'

'Your figures don't add up,' said Lauren, 'that would make a total of six hundred houses in the area.'

'Well, yes, the survey was only an estimate, there could be more or less. So what do you say Miss Holloway? Do we have a deal of some kind? I could collect you on Monday, and we could settle the business within days.'

'First of all, thank you for inviting me to see you,' said Lauren. 'Those trees you mentioned, they have to be uprooted do they?' Ellerslie did not answer, which was an answer in itself. 'Those trees are part of an environmental enhancement present in this area for hundreds of years. They are an ecological pleasure, and host a whole series of species from birds of various types, to squirrels and other animals not to mention a host of insects, all of them beneficial to the environment.' Ellerslie opened his mouth, but Lauren ignored his nascent protest and ploughed on. 'Even if I was amenable to such a desecration of the countryside, there's another question. What will I do with my horses? The meadow is where they can run free in a more natural environment. If you take that away from them they'll have nowhere to go where they can just - play.' She noted that Ellerslie was looking at her with something close to hatred, it was for only a split second, then the professional gloss came back into his manner and he relaxed his features into a calm, urbane expression.

'Now my dear, please come to some arrangement with me. You know very well that the meadows on either side are at the very extremes of both of our properties. I know the size of your estate and the meadow on your side is a fleabite compared with the rest of the property.'

'How do you know the size of my property?' asked Lauren.

'I had a survey done,' said Ellerslie, 'it seemed a waste to commission a civil engineer without getting the whole job done.'

'Strictly speaking, you are guilty of a gross invasion of my business,' said Lauren, sitting forward in her seat, tense and angry.

'Relax my dear, I had your father's permission to do so.'

'I've been looking through his papers; I don't see any permission to do a survey.'

'It was a verbal agreement, a gentleman's handshake, please don't get upset.' Lauren wanted to challenge him on this because she had a feeling that he was being glib, superficial, and he was lying. 'As for your horses, they can 'play' as you call it in other areas of the land, they don't need to be just there. Will you at least think the matter over?`

'I already have,' Lauren got to her feet and started moving towards the door. Ellerslie began to move with her, but she turned on him as quickly as a striking rattlesnake. 'It's all right, I'll see myself out.' He froze on the spot.

'But you haven't answered my question.'

'Yes I have.` She strode to the front door, pulled it wide even as Chivers appeared to do it for her, and swept out into the capacious driveway, jumped into her BMW, switched it on, and did a sweeping turn as the motor roared to life and drove back to Craigton Stables regretting the waste of time.

Chapter Eight

Now, back in the present, she stood there with Yasmin and looked at the letter that promised to do so much to derail her plans for the business. As a lawyer herself, even though she had dealt mainly with contracts and did very little in the way of court work, she knew that being sued was a tricky business. If you did not defend yourself the courts often made some kind of award based on historic precedent. A case could go back many years; it might be that they would force her to sell the land to the builders because it was regarded as important for the district. On the other hand she could defend the case and might well win, but a good lawyer cost a great deal of money. She would be a fool to mount her own defence when this kind of case wasn't her speciality.

'Dammit! He's got me over a barrel; they must be really pressing him to get this deal done. Either way it's going to cost money.'

'Well we'll find a solution,' said Yasmin, 'you know we've always been able to struggle through, we'll find a way.'

'Yes we will,' said Lauren, 'now I have to get to this meeting with Peter, he's promised to put a lot of business my way.' It was on the way out from speaking to Yasmin that she first encountered Nathan.

***

'Please come this way!' the waiter enthused brightly as he ushered Lauren to a table in the restaurant. Nathan followed on, his footfalls firm on the plush carpet behind. But even without the benefit of sound, she'd know he was there, a strange, enticing warmth always accompanied his presence. She felt drawn to its inviting whisper, despite her better judgement.

Lauren gulped dryly as the waiter drew to a halt at a quiet corner and lifted a chair back for her to sit on. She glanced nervously at Nathan and back at the waiter, 'Could we please dine somewhere else?'

Her azure-blue eyes pleaded with him to find them somewhere else, anywhere else to enjoy their meal. She couldn't dream of staying for any length of time in the close intimacy such a setting would nurture; with any other man, yes, but not with Nathan.

"I'm sorry," the waiter replied, smiling widely. "But this is the table Mr King ordered." He looked past her and addressed him, "Isn't that right, sir?"

Lauren turned to face Nathan and balked at the satanic grin playing on his lips. His grey eyes flickered from her surprised expression to the waiter's pleasing smile and back to her again. He winked at her, 'Yes, it's right. And I'm sure the young lady will soon enjoy the benefits of such a learned choice.' He paused to gaze upon her sparkling eyes, and watched intently as she gulped, 'unless she is too afraid of me.'

Lauren bridled at his words. She had never felt afraid of being in any man's presence, and she cursed herself for allowing her mind to turn a mere molehill into another mountain. Time to be herself, the confident, capable businesswoman who could cope with anything life threw at her.

But wasn't that the problem? How could she hope to hold her business persona in such an intimate setting? How could she deal with the prickling discomfort that the drop of business persona into personal persona always instilled in her? She felt safe and secure in business mode and so out of practice with the dating game.

It had been at least two years since she'd dined out with a man, excepting business lunches with clients and those didn't truly count as dates. She felt like a clumsy teenager again and way out of her depth, horribly so.

'You do have a habit of loitering about, don't you?' Nathan commented with a low throaty drawl. His voice penetrated her senses and laid a touch upon her like soft velvet. 'Allow me, Lauren.'

She watched as he gently placed the chair at the table for her to sit on. He swept his arm before her and smiled with glittering eyes, 'Your chair awaits, dear lady!'

Lauren dropped her gaze and hurriedly lowered herself into the chair. She had always been a lover of manners in a man. A soft spot he'd discovered in her with exquisite ease. She steeled herself against her vulnerability, determining not to disclose any more of her soft spots, if she could.

She watched as he sat down in his chair and ordered a bottle of Burgundy. She felt thankful that she could at least have a moment's respite from his attentions. Unable to raise her gaze to him, she placed her handbag by her side and glanced around nervously.

He returned his gaze to her and smiled warmly, 'I must say, you are a very attractive young lady. I feel honoured to be with you.'

Lauren blushed and hurriedly lifted the long-stemmed crystal glass. She sipped at her wine, purposefully avoiding his flattery. Until he grasped the glass from her, and placed it back down upon the table.

'Are you uncomfortable with praise?' he asked, his tone gently probing. 'Such beauty should come hand in hand with pride and an acceptance of admiration.'

'Yes, it should,' she managed to mutter, trying to add an edge to her voice. 'But it isn't something to which I've given much time or attention. How I look has never felt important to me.

Oh, but please don't mistake me. I enjoy being presentable and tidy …'

'As you must,' he responded attentively. 'It's part of your job, one that I know you offer great attention. Appearances are so very influential in business.'

'Yes, they are,' she agreed wholeheartedly, daring to gaze into his face. She had never seen such a piercing quality to a man's eyes, and found it awkward to hold her contact with them. They seemed to strip away her every defence and with such consummate ease she felt driven to wall herself up from him, a protective instinct so alien to her.

'It's a poor business woman who doesn't tend to her appearance.' she continued on, feeling more at ease whilst discussing business affairs.

'Indeed,' he replied, sensing her relax and nodding slowly. 'So how long have you owned your centre? You look almost too young to be in such a position of power.'

Lauren's expression hardened as she corrected him, 'Business isn't all about power, Nathan.' Why the flush of desire when she spoke his name? She could not say. She hurriedly went on, not allowing herself to fathom out the answer. 'It's about people. People shouldn't be so bound up in the power games and struggles that they lose track of the true essence of what it's all about.'

'And what is it all about?' he enquired interestedly, sipping occasionally on his Burgundy, his demeanour a Devil May Care one now, as he openly enjoyed the environment.

His environment, she thought enviously. She felt much more at home out in the countryside amongst the sprawling fields, majestic trees, the fresh scents and sounds of Mother Nature. She wished she could master his ease of being comfortable where ever he may be. But she doubted such a day would come.

'It's about caring for your clients,' she replied softly, thinking how much her parents had instilled such an attitude into her. They had groomed her well in placing the customer first. 'No customer, no business!' they had told her so often that it lay imprinted in her thoughts. 'They are the very essence of business, don't you think?'

'It depends on the customer, I'd say,' he passed comment, his gaze quietly appraising her. She in turn perused him, trying to figure out what he was thinking, but she could tell nothing. The man was so hard to fathom. She sensed much lay hidden beneath his cool, capable exterior, and she could only guess at what. 'I've known some customers that I wouldn't give tuppence for. They acted with a total lack of respect towards me and thought nothing of decrying my obvious and superior knowledge within my business. Instead of listening to me they insisted on replacing my advice with their own egotistical ignorance.' He shrugged his shoulders, 'I mean why do they bother coming to me if they aren't going to listen to me?'

Lauren felt her head nodding without her even thinking about it. The man talked such sense she could do nothing but agree with him. She, too, had experienced such customers. The Know-It-Alls who didn't know anything.

But they had still lined her bank account, and done so, so well, she'd learned to nurture a dogged tolerance of them. After all, business came first. No room for personal feelings.

'What's your business?' she asked Nathan, a twinge of curiosity tugging at her. She felt sure he owned a business of some sort or other. He looked a wealthy man not afraid to flaunt his success.

'I'm a course-builder for eventing competitions,' he replied obligingly. 'It's a most fascinating occupation that has allowed me to travel all over the world; from the US to New Zealand to Germany. Travel so enriches one's life, don't you think?'

'It does,' she replied, fighting hard to stem the strong feeling of rapport that rose within her at his admission of being involved in the horse business. So strong the surge, she had to quickly drop her gaze and look away.

Good Lord! she thought, handsome, wealthy and a lover of horses. The man was a dream come true. She couldn't count the number of times she'd dreamt of such a man. And now he was sitting before. More real and excitingly handsome than any man she had ever seen.

The men she'd previously dated had all been gold-diggers as far as she could see, and men who had wickedly faked their love of horses in an attempt to soften her affections. But so deep was her love of horses, she'd picked up on their insincerity almost instantly, and sent them packing.

She didn't sense such insincerity in Nathan. Even in the briefest of references to his occupation, his tone had been genuine and laced with a flattering acknowledgement and appreciation of the perks he'd received.

'Hello … hello?' his voice sounded in her ears. She felt his fingers tapping lightly on her forehead. 'Is anyone at home?'

Lauren chuckled softly. 'I'm sorry … I drifted off for a moment.'

'Yes, you did,' he replied smoothly. He looked at her, an eyebrow rising questioningly. 'And where did you drift off to, I wonder?' The corners of his slim lips turned upwards, his grey eyes glittered knowingly. 'I'm sure it was pleasant where ever it was.'

She blushed. An uncomfortable blush he couldn't draw his eyes from. Her flesh felt aflame under his intense scrutiny.

'Wh .. when is the waiter taking our order?' she stuttered, loathing being so naked to him. She felt like the silly naïve teenager again, and longed to be away from him. Just for a few moments … just to draw the breath into her body … just to clear her thoughts … just to be the businesswoman.

Just to be safe from him.

'It shan't be long now,' he reassured her, thankfully breaking his gaze to call the waiter over.

The man finished serving his customer and attended to Nathan immediately. Lauren felt impressed by the man's response. She had rarely witnessed such quick service, but she guessed that he only responded as he had with special customers, of which Nathan was one. 'I have to make a phone call right now. I shouldn't be long but please go ahead and take the lady's order. I'll have my usual.'

'Certainly, sir,' he smiled back, standing to wait for Lauren's order as Nathan excused himself and strode out to the foyer.

Lauren breathed a sigh of relief that a simple phone call would allow her time to regroup before the continuation of their evening. She felt as though she was walking on eggshells. She was so confident discussing business, yet still yearning to relax more in his presence.

But she couldn't allow herself such a luxury. It had taken all her strength to keep him at arm's length. For her to choose to relax would be for her to choose to open her heart to him. And this she just couldn't allow.

Lauren found that being left alone with her thoughts proved worse than being in Nathan's company. She found herself wondering madly about him. Did he have a wife? Or was he single? And if he was single, why? It was because handsome wealthy men were few and far between in her experience.

Not that she had much experience. It consisted of a handful of light, brief affairs bereft of the caring and deep love that should be such an important part of a relationship.

They had left her feeling empty and dissatisfied, and even more determined to plough all her energy and time into the centre. Nothing in her life made her feel as alive and invigorated than her centre.

'I'm sorry about that.' Nathan said, as he rejoined her. 'Peter asked for some details that I didn't have available for him at the meeting earlier.'

'So you were unprepared?' Lauren said, grinning mischievously at him. 'Bad business practice, you know.'

Nathan laughed readily, his grey eyes twinkling with mirth. 'Yes, I'm afraid this time you're right. But I can defer this error to my secretary as she didn't include the figures I asked for. Still, not to mind, it's all remedied and Peter is quite happy.'

Lauren wondered why Peter was happy and why Nathan was the cause of it. What did he have to do with her client? They seemed to know each other quite well from what she could tell, and she found a myriad of questions appearing, searching for their answers.

How long had they known each other? Had they been in business together? And if so, what kind of business? Long-term or short-term? What type of business were they conducting now?

She longed to ask him but thought better of it. She didn't want to appear nosy, best to just try and enjoy the evening.

'So you're not of winning material, you say?' he asked, his grey eyes sparkling with interest.

'No, far from it, I'm afraid,' she replied, not too proud to admit that she would never reach the standards needed to fly with the elite of the eventing world. 'Jewel and I recognised our failings very soon into competing. She's a dream ride but she isn't very good at concentrating. Her mind wanders when it shouldn't.'

He smiled and drawled, 'Not unlike her owner. Hmmm?'

Lauren nodded abashed. 'Now there's a thought! It maybe isn't Jewel, after all. The problem possibly lies with me.'

He tutted before, 'No 'possibly' about it, I'd say. The responsibility of holding the animal's attention lies solely with the rider. If the rider isn't finding enough to keep her attention, then why would she expect the horse to be interested? The essence of good course-building … keeping the attention of the rider and inviting the horse into a welcoming fence.'

Lauren felt herself nodding subconsciously again, 'Yes, you're so right. So many riders just let their thoughts wander sometimes.'

'And where did yours wander off to, I wonder?' he mused, the glint of suggestiveness causing her to take a quick sip of her wine. Why did her lips feel so dry? Why did her heart pound so wildly at his forwardness?

I'm just out of practice, she reassured herself. This dating lark just needs getting accustomed to again and then it would be as easy as pie. She couldn't foresee herself reaching the masterly dating prowess of the man before her, but that wasn't her aim. Her aim was to try and retain what little composure she was hanging on to.

'I tried not to let them wander,' she replied, replacing her wine glass on the crisp white tablecloth. 'But Jewel takes a lot of handling at the best of times …'

'Stop blaming your poor mare,' he stated reproaching her, his gaze direct and sure. 'You are the one in charge, and maybe if you'd learned to acknowledge your fault more, you would've fared much better in your competitive life. Blame yourself and improve yourself. And your horse will show the best of its ability. It's not unlike a fine car. The more experienced the person driving, the better the performance. Now take the lesson and learn to improve.'

Lauren felt his words prickle like red-hot cinders on her skin. How quickly he swung from being complimentary and knowledgeable to adopting the teacher stance with her. It irritated her beyond belief.

"Listen," she said, glowering across the table at him as he mischievously cocked his head at her. She ignored his attempt at consolidating her ire and continued, "I don't much care for your wiseass remarks, either on a personal or professional basis!"

He leant forward and slowly slipped his fingers upon her own, she fought hard against her instinct to pull away from the burning sensation his touch always stirred. She instead stayed as still as her trembling would permit. He gazed deep into her eyes and whispered softly, 'I haven't started becoming personal with you yet, Lauren.'

Lauren gulped dryly and dropped her gaze. Her face felt as though it was aflame. She couldn't bear for him to look upon her warmed flesh. He would but warm it more.

He squeezed her hand gently and stroked it with such tenderness; she felt a tremor of excitement shiver over her skin. She desired so much to raise her gaze to him but could only stare spellbound at the long delicate fingers stroking her with such raw masculinity.

'The waiter at last!' he spoke aloud, breaking his grasp and leaving Lauren with a horrible feeling of coldness. His skin had no sooner left her own until she'd longed for him to touch her once more. She dared to raise her gaze and sat entranced at the vision of the man. He felt incredibly dangerous and attracted her so powerfully; she could hardly hear herself draw breath.

Lauren couldn't wait for the evening to end.

Chapter Nine

'Thank you for a pleasant evening,' Lauren said quietly, as Nathan slowed the Mercedes to a halt outside her single-level cottage. 'I really enjoyed myself.'

'It was my pleasure, Lauren,' he replied, his tone showing he was pleased at her words. 'We must do it again sometime soon.'

He slowly turned to face her but she couldn't match his gaze. The interior of the car felt suffocating, far too warm. Just raising her eyes and looking upon him fired her desire. She prayed that he wouldn't lay his touch on her but …

Without warning, Nathan reached towards her and slipped his forefinger under her chin. He gently coaxed her face round to his own and gazed deeply into her eyes. His breath swept on her lips … warm and cold … his scent tangy and male.

Her soft pink lips parted unbidden and she couldn't … wouldn't surrender to her desire to pull away from him. She craved the feel of his hard mouth on her own. She longed to taste him …

Nathan placed a gentle kiss on her slightly moist lips. A kiss so light and fleeting, she felt somehow cheated.

'Now go and rest,' he drawled huskily, drawing his finger from her chin. 'You have a busy time beginning what with all your bookings. It wouldn't do you any good to be tired at such a time. A tired businesswoman often makes more mistakes than a refreshed one.'

Lauren wanted to tell him that she knew the basic facts of running a business, but all she could think of was how cold the evening had become. The time for parting had arrived, and from fighting against his initial invite, she now longed for it to continue.

Tap, tap, tap, his fingers were playing on her forehead once more. She'd drifted off so easily, she hadn't even feel herself going.

'You really do linger a lot, don't you?' he commented warmly, smiling affectionately at her. 'Not that I mind, of course, but I do have an early rise tomorrow.'

'Oh, I'm sorry,' she apologised, feeling she'd suddenly overstayed her welcome. 'Thank you for the dinner and goodnight, Nathan.'

'Goodnight, Lauren,' he replied, watching as she opened the door to leave. 'Sleep well and sweet dreams.'

She glanced back at him, 'You can be sure of the dreams …'

A mischievous glint appeared in his grey eyes and she instantly bit her lip. Damn, did she have to be so obvious?

As if she could help herself, she thought. He made her feel like a teenager. And she loved the sensation. No man had ever evoked such desire in her so instantly.

She rose from the car-seat and closed the door. She made her way to the oak door of the cottage and turned to wave him away.

Within a few moments, he was gone. And Lauren suddenly felt the chill of the night air blanket down on her warmed flesh.

Then she heard the ring of her home phone sound indoors.

She quickly unlocked the door and entered the cottage.

'Hang on! I'm coming!' she called, despite the caller not being able to hear. She lifted the receiver, 'Hello, Lauren here. Who's speaking?'

'It's Yasmin,' her secretary's voice sounded. There was a distinct edge of excitement and apprehension in her voice, one that felt strange. The edge she heard when Yasmin fell prone to reluctant gossiping. 'I've some news for you. It's about Nathan.'

Pleased that her assessment had proven right, Lauren asked, 'What about him?'

'Do you remember the Borders incident? It's years ago now..'

'Of course I do. Who could forget? Poor Buck was killed.'

'Yes well,' Yasmin continued cautiously, knowing the effect her news would have on her boss, but feeling it her duty to disclose her information regardless of the predicted reaction. 'Nathan is the saboteur ...'

'No!' Lauren burst out loudly. 'It can't be true. Please tell me you're joking, Yasmin. Please!'

'I'm not joking,' she replied. 'Mr Thompson told me when he called by the office to drop off the bill for Jade's treatment. He said that he'd met him down at the stables and chatted with him briefly. He said that Nathan changed his name shortly before he left for the United States. That's the reason you didn't recognise him.'

'Mr Thompson might be mistaken,' Lauren projected hopefully, though acknowledging that he was rarely wrong about anything in his life. He was an excellent judge of character and fell party to most of the gossip of the horse world. 'The last I heard of Nathan he'd left the country to escape the shame of being ostracised from eventing circles. Why would he come back to England and why so soon? The Borders incident happened only three years ago.'

'Maybe he thinks we all have short memories,' she replied suggestively. 'Or maybe he just wants to have a second chance. Everyone deserves a second chance. No matter what ill deed or crime they've committed.'

Lauren couldn't believe her ears. 'Well, you do have a short memory, don't you? The man is responsible for loosing off poles from a cross-country fence and allowing them to come to rest on the landing area. Right where poor Buck's hooves came down.

The terrified animal had no safe place to land. The witnesses told the inquiry that it was one of the worst falls they'd ever seen on an eventing course. And as for Kay, his rider, she was lucky to survive the horror. She couldn't even stay with Buck whilst the vet put him to sleep. Nathan could've killed them both.'

'But he didn't,' Yasmin ventured bravely. She knew how strongly Lauren had reacted to the original telling of the Borders story, and it seemed that time had not lessened her rage at the man responsible. 'And he publicly expressed his regret to Kay about what had happened. He showed great remorse.'

Lauren scoffed loudly, 'And Buck still lay cold and dead as Kay broke her heart on my shoulder. She's never recovered from her loss. I met her just last week. She invited me along to watch her school a new gelding she's just bought.' Shock hit at her senses. 'Good Lord, how is it going to look if she discovers Nathan is here?'

Lauren felt her throat dry uncomfortably. It didn't bear thinking about.

The distant sound of a familiar BMW engine sounded in her ears. Good Lord, he's coming back! she thought horrified.

'Look, Yasmin,' she said quickly, trying to keep the nervousness from her voice and failing. 'I have to go. He's returning.'

'Are you going to be all right?' she asked, her voice quivering with apprehension. 'I could send young Tom round if you want, if you're too scared to open the door.'

'No!' she shot back, trying to breathe slow and relaxed. 'I'll be fine. I'm not going to open the door to him. I'm just going to find out what he wants and then tell him to leave and never come back.'

She bade Yasmin a swift 'goodbye' and replaced the receiver just as three knocks thudded down hard on the oak door.

'What do you want, Nathan?' she asked coldly, grateful for the protection of the door. Her heart pounded hard in her chest. Her fingers trembled as she held the door-handle.

'I'd like to speak with you face to face if it's not too much bother,' he replied, bewildered. He rapped his knuckles on the door again, causing her to jump at the unexpectedness. 'It's rather silly of us to be chatting through a door after having spent such a nice evening together.'

No, it isn't silly at all, she thought sensibly. She had him exactly where she wanted him and wasn't prepared to budge an inch.

'Look, just tell me why you're here and then we can both say 'goodbye' to each other!'

'Goodbye?' he asked amazed. 'Why would I want to say goodbye to you? We've only just met.' He grasped the door-handle and rattled it, 'Now open up or …'

'No, I won't!' she shouted back at him, angry at her loss of control. She could count on the fingers of one hand how often she'd raised her voice to anyone. She preferred the quiet, tactful approach. 'So why don't you just turn and leave me alone? I don't want you here. Go away!'

All fell quiet. Lauren hoped he'd gone but knew he hadn't. She had heard no footfalls crunching upon the gravel, no car door shutting, no engine starting, no car drawing down the driveway. He was still there, a mass of confused and angry masculinity.

'Do you use your mobile phone much, Lauren?' his voice eventually sounded.

'What is it to you? Yes, I use it for taking calls when I'm out working my centre,' she replied, curious as to his new line of conversation. What the blazes did her phone have to do with anything? What a strange tangent. Maybe he was trying to confuse her so that she would open the door. He would be wasting his time. 'I couldn't be without it.'

'That's fine,' he went on. 'I'll just keep it then. If you start missing it, you can call and we can make arrangements for you to uplift it. That is, if I haven't thrown it in the rubbish bin first, of course. You see, I can't use a phone I have no pin number for.'

'You have my phone?' she asked sharply, almost duped into unlocking the door but checking herself at the last minute.

No answer. Just the familiar ring tone of her mobile. Damn the man! She thought angrily.

'You hand that back right now!' she shouted at him, wishing she was standing beside him glaring into his eyes. 'It belongs to me, you thief!'

'No, it used to belong to you,' he replied with cold logic. 'And now it belongs to me to do with as I will. Finders keepers, losers weepers, I believe that old, but oh so true saying goes.'

She heard his harsh, mocking laugh resound in her ears. Unable to resist the overpowering impulse to rebuke him, she unlocked the door and threw it wide open.

'You give it back right now!' she glared hard at him, her chin held up defiantly. 'Or I shall report you to the police.'

He shrugged his shoulders, 'Your choice. I'll simply explain to them that I called back to return it to you. My motives were honourable.'

'Honourable!' she shot back, her anger nipping at her like bee-stings. She had never felt so enraged. 'And what would someone like you know about a quality such as honour? You're a damn hypocrite!'

The lean angles of his face sharpened, his eyebrows lowered and cast menacing shadows in his grey eyes. She watched anxiously as his whole body tensed. Good Lord, what had she stirred? Why hadn't she just opened the door, accepted the kind return of her phone and bid him goodnight?

Because she now hated the very sight of him, she thought, hackles rising on the back of her neck.

'Just what in the name of hell has got into you, lady?' he snarled nastily, his white teeth showing through tight lips. 'I dropped you off less than ten minutes ago. And in that short time, you've turned from the most exquisite creature into a rabid wildcat. What's wrong with you?'

'With me!' she threw back, aghast at the nerve of the man. 'I'm not the one with the problem. I actually care. And a lot more than you ever did, you murdering brute!'

Nathan shook his head disbelievingly, 'I'll tell you what, lady.' He stepped towards her and she bravely held her ground. 'You just take your phone back and we'll make out that tonight never happened!' He grasped her hand and slapped the phone into the palm of her hand, 'There! You be sure and sleep well now!'

He turned quickly away and strode towards the big black BMW. A few seconds later and he had gone.

Chapter Ten

It was the next day, in the morning, in the office.

'You did what?' Lauren asked Yasmin astonished, glaring at her with a fierce intensity she rarely had to use on her secretary. What a terrible start to the morning!

'I booked Nathan in for ten o'clock,' she replied, unable to face the glare. Her nature was one of a peacemaker and she loathed and avoided open confrontation of any kind. A trait that Lauren didn't possess. 'I thought …'

'No, you didn't think!' Lauren continued her onslaught, breaking her gaze to pace up and down the office floor. 'If you'd thought, I wouldn't be in this mess. What on earth am I going to say to my clients if … no, when they discover I have horse-killer training at my centre?'

'You shouldn't call him that,' Yasmin replied cautiously. She had watched Lauren in such moods before and understood that it wouldn't be the best time to press her opinions. But she couldn't help herself. 'People can't trail their past mistakes along with them everywhere they go.'

'And Nathan has travelled well to avoid this particular mistake,' Lauren fumed, feeling driven to vent on Yasmin. She could have put paid to the business of goodness knows how many of her clients. And it couldn't have happened at a worst time.

'Who knows what awful deeds he's perpetrated under his pseudonym?'

Yasmin shook her head, 'I think you're being too harsh on him. He seemed pleasant enough when I spoke with him, very pleasant indeed.'

Lauren stopped pacing and turned to face her secretary; just as she thought, Yasmin's normally demure expression was dreamy and her skin positively glowing.

Damn the man! She thought disgustedly. Did he always find it so easy to turn female heads? They must fall at his feet in droves. And hadn't she done the same? It piqued her to acknowledge that she had.

'Well, there's no point in saying any more,' she continued, hoping to thwart Nathan's arrival at her centre.

'And you do tell me to accept as many bookings as possible,' Yasmin went on, ignoring her boss's words. 'I was just doing what you asked me to do.'

'Within reason,' Lauren retorted sharply, not quite believing her secretary's defence. 'I didn't mean you should accept known killers …'

'Ah but I didn't know who he was until Mr Thompson told me and that was after the booking.' she expertly defended herself, forcing Lauren to accept the facts of the matter.

'Okay, I agree,' she responded fairly. 'You're correct. You didn't and couldn't have known, but I now have to contact Nathan and stop him keeping the booking. And I need to do it before any more clients arrive. Do you have his phone number?'

Yasmin glanced at the wall-clock, 'It doesn't matter if I have or haven't, it's five minutes to ten. He'll be arriving shortly.'

Lauren spun round and stared at the clock. Good grief! He could be on the grounds right now. Anywhere! Talking to anyone! Ruining her reputation!

'Oh Yasmin!' she exploded, panic-stricken. 'Now I have to go searching for him. He could be anywhere.'

'Surely he'd go to the trailer park first.'

'I do hope so!'

***

Nathan couldn't be seen anywhere. The park had two trailers and she recognised both; one belonged to Mrs Cassidy and the other to Ursula.

She breathed a quiet sigh of relief, knowing that they hadn't seen Nathan. Or at least not that she knew of, panic setting it again.

Ursula waved to Lauren and she waved back. She longed to go and ask her if she'd seen Nathan around, but she knew she wasn't the one to ask. Her nature was the opposite of Yasmin's and she loved nothing better than some juicy gossip to spread around.

Lauren hoped she'd set her sights on Nathan long before Ursula did or the whole of Scotland would know about her predicament by lunchtime.

She hurriedly stopped her thoughts wandering off into awful possibilities and concentrated on solving her problem. It's what she happened to be good at, after all. She'd had to be a problem-solver. It was part and parcel of running her own business.

Now where could he be? First stop would be the park and he wasn't there. Next?

She couldn't think of "next". It was the only place he could park the trailer as there would be no parking space on the roads surrounding the stables. They comprised of a narrow country road and a dual carriageway.

Maybe he hasn't made it, she thought hopefully.

No, she immediately retracted her guesswork. He was the type to complete everything he said he was going to do. She was certain he would be somewhere on the estate, somewhere. But where?

A thought suddenly struck Lauren. What if he didn't need a trailer to arrive? What if he'd hacked over on his mount? It would explain the missing trailer.

And she knew that Mr Young, her next door neighbour, offered half and full livery at his farm to boost his income.

How she hoped that wasn't where Nathan was stabling his horse. It felt too close for comfort. Much too close!

A whinny sounded in the distance. It sounded strange and not one that she recognised. There were only two clients on her land at the moment and she knew their horses' whinnies.

It must be Nathan's mount, she thought relieved. And even if it wasn't, it still called for her to investigate. It wouldn't be the first time that one of Mr Young's horses had accidentally strayed on to her land. His fencing had been torn down during a terrible storm last summer and his stray horses, being the naturally inquisitive and roaming creatures they are, had all decided to visit her centre.

There had been five strays, and after breaking through into her woodland ride, they had encroached on her jumping course. She balked at the thought of what may have happened if there had been riders on her course at such a crucially dangerous time.

The last thing a rider wanted to see as they were cantering into a jump was a stray horse dart out at them from nowhere. The horse being ridden usually spooked badly; and it would be an expert rider who would be able to stay put in such circumstances. Most fell off due to the sudden, unexpected swerve away from the stray horse, usually having the misfortune to land on the hard upper pole of the jump.

So, she must go and check out the situation anyway. Besides, time was running out before the trailers started arriving. Speed was of the essence.

The whinny sounded deep in the woodland once more, and knowing it would be some time before she reached the source of the noise if she walked, and knowing that the rider most probably wouldn't stay in the same spot for long, she decided it would make sense for her to saddle up Jewel and ride instead. Lauren's centre covered over seventy acres, and it wouldn't be easy to cover the ground needed by walking.

'Stop right where you are!' Lauren shouted loudly, watching Nathan stride purposefully towards a small wooden jumping fence. But he strode on, oblivious to her call. Or ignoring it.

'Hey there! Stop in your tracks!' she shouted louder, desperation creeping into her voice. Good grief, the nerve of the man. Sabotaging her fences in broad daylight. The man had no shame or discretion.

She halted Jewel and dismounted. After quickly securing the reins to a post, she strode over to him. Her plait swung angrily behind, her azure-blue eyes were ablaze. She felt every nerve in her body tingling with nervous anticipation. She was, after all, in the middle of a woodland glade with a horse-killer.

'Who are you shouting at?' Nathan asked coldly, his brows casting dark shadows in his eyes. His lips were set hard in a line of defiance. He stood facing her with his hands resting on his hips. His almost nonchalant air edged Lauren's anger up a notch or two, despite her attempts at staying in control. 'The whole centre will hear you, for crying out loud. What do you want?'

'My horses and riders walking about fit and healthy at the end of the training day,' she replied coldly, fighting against the impulse to shove him away from the fence. It wouldn't be a wise move on her part to physically challenge him because she felt his superior strength would easily surpass her own. It would be best on her part to attempt the mental approach.

'I know who you are, Nathan. And I don't want to see you anywhere near my centre, let alone my fences. So I would be grateful if you would just mount your horse...'

'Shadow,' he interrupted shortly, nodding over to a sleek black thoroughbred tied to a thick low-hanging branch. He was a beautiful animal, toned muscles rippling as he scraped the dirt with impatience. He snorted and tossed his head in the air, keen to return to his outing.

'Shadow,' she said obligingly, drawing her gaze from the tempestuous stallion. 'I want you to mount Shadow and leave immediately.'

'Oh you do, do you?' he glared blackly, staring so intently into her eyes she felt he could read her every thought. Convincing herself that he couldn't, enough to at least gather herself even to speak coherently, she nodded at him, 'and your reason for asking me to leave?'

'I've already answered you. I know your identity and you don't belong here.'

He turned from her, and made his way to the side of the fence. He leant down and pulled a yellow plant from the ground. He strode angrily towards her and held it up to her face, 'And neither should this! Do you know what it is, woman? And what it can do to your horses if they ingest it?'

Lauren gulped dryly. His close proximity felt both scary and exciting. And she couldn't make her mind up as to what was causing what. His eyes bore down hard on her, his lips .. lips she could hardly draw her eyes from .. were set firm as he waited for her response. Lauren felt the familiar flush of warmth sweep over her skin.

But now wasn't the time to acknowledge the strange feelings he stirred so readily within her. He looked fit to kill.

'It's called ragwort,' she replied knowledgeably, raising her head and staring at him defiantly. 'And yes I know that it could potentially kill one of my horses ...'

'Or all of them. How many more of these yellow perils do you have growing around your land?'

Lauren momentarily bit her lip. She would have to learn to count to ten with this man as he triggered rage in her so easily. That was another useful addition to her 'Things to learn list.

'I don't see that I have to answer to you!' she threw back, steeling herself to look into his glittering grey eyes. His gaze made her feel naked, emotionally and physically. But she would learn to face up to his gaze whether it took her the rest of her life or not.

'You've nothing to do with my business. And will soon be having less to do with it,' she added firmly, reminding him that his imminent departure from her land hadn't slipped off the agenda. 'But I'll humour you for now. I'd guess there would be very few. I send my staff out regularly to clear out poisonous plants. They do so at least every two or three weeks.'

He scoffed loudly and said, 'Then they aren't doing a very good job of eradicating the problem, are they?' He suddenly grasped her wrist.

Lauren's heart thudded noisily. Her skin burned with his touch. His fingers felt like a vice of steel as he walked her over to the fence. She tried to struggle free, unable to stand the dizziness his touch evoked within her. But his fingers were strong and determined.

He stopped beside the right-hand side of the fence and pointed at the fresh bare earth disturbed by his uprooting of the ragwort plant. 'How could any one of your staff miss it if it's so damn near your fence? Even if it was missed on the poison eradication trips they did, the person who's maintaining the fence should have spotted it and yanked it out!'

Lauren felt such rage roar through her on hearing his words that she found the energy to struggle free of his firm grasp. She lifted her hand and tried to rub away the heat of her skin, but always managed in heating it further. Good Lord, this man felt dangerous. Never before had she felt so affected by a man's touch. What was happening to her?

'Who the hell are you to be standing there talking to me about fence maintenance, you hypocrite!' she shot back, trying hard to concentrate on the task at hand. And finding it so difficult.

Those dark eyes bore hard into her, making her own gaze pale into nothing. A light breeze ruffled his black hair, setting her nerves tingling uncontrollably. His lean and muscular physique stirred such desire within her that she longed to run her fingers over every hard line and soft curve.

'Hypocrite?' he threw back, almost nonchalantly. She watched as the corner of his lips curved slightly, balked at the dark glint in his eyes. Had he picked up on her desire? Had she been so obvious to him once more?

He grabbed hold of her with lean, strong hands, a hard, rough pull into his body confirmed she had. His lean, masculine physique melded against her own so easily, she felt instinctively drawn to yield to him. But she steeled herself.

'Would you like to kiss a hypocrite?' he drawled huskily, his hot, slightly spicy breath brushing upon her slightly parted mouth. Her lips felt dry but she fought against the temptation to moisten them with her tongue. She instinctively sensed he would perceive her licking as an invite. The last thing she wanted or needed was to be openly provocative.

He paused tantalisingly, waiting for her answer but her words would not come. She could hardly draw breath, let alone form words in her thoughts and speak them.

She had come here to be rid of him, to chase him off her land in order to safeguard her business. Where had all her motivation gone? She knew what could happen if the trainers and riders, soon to be arriving at her centre saw her anywhere near him, let alone condoning his presence on her land, let alone allowing him to ravish her.

But every part of her wanted to tell him that she wanted his kiss, the feel of his hard male mouth on her lips, the lean firmness of his body against her own.

Excruciatingly slowly, he lowered his lips to her own waiting mouth. Her thoughts spun crazily in anticipation. Her blood pulsed wildly in her throat. Her breath caught in short gasps.

'Yes, you do, don't you?' he whispered huskily, stopping but a breath from her lips. 'You want so much more than last evening.' He paused for what felt like a tortuous eternity. Then in one swift action, he pushed her away.

Lauren felt the heat of the moment burn. It didn't matter that he'd pushed her from him. It made no difference to her body at all; just laying her eyes upon him set her desire aflame.

'I admire a woman who can stick to her principles,' he said mockingly, running a lazy gaze up and down her trembling body. He threw the ragwort at her feet, 'Burn it! It's the only way to be truly rid of it.' He nodded at the spot where he'd found the plant and sneered, 'Check out for any seed-heads that may be lying about before you go!'

Lauren felt her head spinning. He was speaking to her so harshly about business that had nothing to do with him, ordering her to pull weeds on her own land. Angry words vied for position but for the life of her, she couldn't speak them.

Instead, she watched dumbfounded as he strode towards his steed, mount up and leave. She felt the familiar coldness fall upon her skin as she clung to and watched the last glimpse of Shadow and his rider disappear into the woodland.

Still entranced by the spell, her fingers lifted, unbidden, to her mouth. She slowly touched lips denied the warmth of his kiss. She sensed the beginning.

Chapter Eleven

The phone call was unexpected. He asked her to go with him to Edinburgh for the new horse show taking place there. He had a major part in designing the event. As he would be away for a few days he wanted company, and besides, he had a few clients he wanted to meet. He would be fine if he was alone, but would look much better for him if he was accompanied by a pleasing companion. Would she like to be his escort?

He hastened to add this was more in the nature of business than personal, and he would make sure her employees were paid for any overtime to cover her while she was away. At first Lauren was faintly insulted by his approach. Business indeed! Then she put on her thinking cap and realised that if this trip was indeed as important to him as he was implying, then perhaps, in his own way he was complimenting her by asking her to go with him.

There was the question of Buck, the dead horse in the Borders event, and his injured rider Kay. Could she really put her feelings of outrage at that situation aside and spend time with a man who had committed such a heinous act? Yet he didn't seem to think that he had done anything to be ashamed of. He had changed his name, but that seemed to be for business purposes only because he clearly wasn't ashamed to be here.

The hell with it! He piqued her curiosity, she wanted to get to the bottom of the matter and find out what had really happened. Besides he was offering her a free trip, all expenses paid, and she hadn't done anything fresh for years. She simply didn't have enough money left over from paying wages and running costs to do such a thing,

She had a few smart clothes in her wardrobe left over from her days in Edinburgh, it would be nice to visit the old place again, and thanks to working every day in the stables, she not only fitted into her old dresses, she was trimmer than when she was a budding lawyer. Finally she called him back and said 'yes.' As she put the phone down she was surprised to find her heart was hammering a little. It was only business, that's all it was. Or so she told herself.

***

The Edinburgh Equine Show was the kind of event she hadn't been to for a few years. It was held in the Edinburgh indoor athletics arena. Suddenly Lauren felt nervous, even as the car drew up to the entrance of the huge indoor space. She had been there in the past, but had been so busy building up her own business that she had forgotten how imposing the place was. The entrance was decorated with flags of a few nations, including Italy, France, Germany, and of course the United Kingdom.

'They're putting on a good show already,' said Nathan easily turning, his large vehicle into the car park, which was thronged with some especially upmarket motors. He casually drove his BMW into one of the VIP areas, and was met with a gentleman in red, white and blue livery who was obviously one of the many paid attendants policing the event.

'Here pal,' said the man, 'this bit's reserved for the nobs.' Lauren presumed he meant the word as shorthand for 'nobility,' or maybe he was just being rude, the slightest hint of power could do that to some people.

'Maybe I should show you my pass,' said Nathan, jumping lithely out of the car while Lauren emerged hastily on the other side. She looked remarkably pretty, wearing a rich red summer dress that fluttered in the breeze, the hat on her head the same inviting red, along with the clutch purse that she carried. Nathan took out a laminated pass, and displayed considerable restraint as he showed it to the man, who waited with a faintly insulting air. She knew it wasn't beneath Nathan to take a pot shot at someone who was being so objectionable and she wanted to avoid a scene on this, her first big day out with the man who was her escort. Hers! As she looked at Nathan's handsome profile in the summer light she experienced a thrill passing through her body that was so powerful she felt dizzy, and thought she was going to pass out. There was no mistaking what she was feeling, a wave of lust was passing through her body, making her breasts tingle, and other parts of her body too. She did not know why she felt such a sudden erotic charge; perhaps it was because her handsome man was quietly simmering with barely concealed rage at being challenged by a flunky.

'Nathan King?' grunted the attendant, 'never heard of you, what makes you so special?'

'Nothing makes me particularly special;' said Nathan, 'but for some reason the organisers seem to be making a bit of a fuss over me.' He looked pointedly at the large billboard behind the man. They were all so close that the words stuck out in red: 'Nathan King, arena course designer.' The flunky turned beetroot red with embarrassment, handing Nathan the card back, hurrying off without looking back.

'I'm proud of you,' said Lauren grabbing him by the arm, resisting the urge to hug him as they made their way to the main entrance. 'I thought you were going to paste him for his insolence.'

'The man was doing his job,' said Nathan, 'and when you think about it, it's a rubbish task looking after a car park during one of these big international shows. Besides, I have a lot bigger fish to fry than some jobs worth worrying about where I park my car.' He did not elaborate on this, but Lauren had a sudden flash of insight. Although he was well-dressed, tall, outwardly confident, even smiling at the people he met on the way in, Nathan was nervous.

Nervous? It did not seem possible, but then she had yet another insight. This was his first British-based show since the humiliation of a few years before.

She realised too that it was not the humiliation that was the primary cause of his disquiet, but the way a rider had been badly injured, while Buck, the horse, had been killed during a show for which he was responsible.

Once they were through the grand entrance they were whisked away to the VIP section by a tall, elderly gentleman who introduced himself as the chairman of the eventing committee. From then on Lauren found herself with Nathan in a square surrounded by long tables groaning with food and drink, and where liveried waiters poured champagne and presented it to the esteemed guests on silver trays. Not being much of a drinker Lauren declined the siren call of the bubbly, and also the lure of the canapés and salmon sandwiches. She felt faintly sick with a combination of excitement and dread, sticking with Evian water in a tall glass garnished with a slice of lemon. She noticed that Nathan did the same, while making sure that he circulated and spoke to as many people as possible. Before leaving her side he put his arm around her waist and gave her a squeeze that again made her tingle with excitement.

'I hate this bloody part of the job,' he muttered, his hot breath close to her ear, 'but it's necessary to keep the work rolling in. I've been on committees with half these people for the last month.' He put on his seemingly easy smile and left her side. Lauren, left to her own devices went over to the arena and had a good look at the presentation of the new fences.

With money to spend, and his career at stake, Nathan had taken the bold step of modelling the periphery of the fences on famous Scottish castles. She could see representations of Shambellie House (which was a type of castle), Culzean Castle, and half a dozen more, all flanking the carefully constructed poles and supports that made up the jumping part of the display. The piece de resistance was of course a representation of Edinburgh Castle, which made up the décor of the final, most difficult jump, across from which was the judges table, giving them an eyeful of the finale.

The main arena was already filled, and there was a sound in the air, a sort of indefinable buzz that came from thousands of people all talking at once, uplifting the whole event. Classical music was playing over the sound system, but at a volume that was far from disturbing to the ear. She recognised one or two pieces by Strauss including the 'Blue Danube' and the music helped to soothe her nerves a little, along with just being here and feeling that she was part of something so huge.

'Penny for them,' said a voice at her ear, and Nathan was at her side, looking at the main arena and the jumps that he had so painstakingly designed. Lauren was filled with an almost overwhelming need to ask him to take her away somewhere out of sight and make love to her; such were the feelings that throbbed within her still young, lustful body. He put his arm around her waist and she returned the favour. The pair of them looked a natural fit, standing there and taking in the atmosphere. At least she was, his feelings manifested themselves in a low whistle that he tended to use to vent his feelings when he was stressed. It was an unconscious way he had of letting off steam, perhaps?

'I'm consciously fighting against the urge to go out there one more time and inspect every single one of those fences,' he said. 'This is a deal breaker for me; I've been given a chance at the very top of the game, if this one blows up my career is over.' Then he squeezed her again and she felt as if she was going to faint from excitement. 'You know what? I just hope none of the horses - or riders come to think of it - get injured, that would be more than I could bear.'

This was rich, she thought, for a man who had been accused of sabotaging his own event in a former life, maybe it was a kind of verbal hypocrisy? The thought of the poor horse and rider made her pull away from him, and suddenly her desire diminished. She did not know if she could trust this man who had shown his arrogance to her before.

The socialising over, it was time for them to take their seats. They were of course at the very front of the action in some of the best seats in the house. They could have elected to go into a special hospitality box with some VIP's, but Nathan had chosen a ringside seat, not wanting either of them to be removed in any way from the action.

There was a blaring of trumpets from the sound system, the announcement that the competition was about to begin, and for spectators to remain quiet. Suddenly, the atmosphere in the building changed. There was no silence of course; because in such a big place even the breathing of thousands was a sound in itself, and there was always some residual muttering in the background, but this was now a theatrical performance of the first magnitude.

Then the first horse and rider came trotting into the arena, and the spectacle began. Although she was still acutely aware of the magnificent man beside her, and the way her body tingled whenever she felt his touch - and they were so closely seated that his left leg would touch her thigh - Lauren found that she was drawn to the spectacle more than ever before. It was that combination of man or woman, and horse, the sound of hoofs dancing across the arena, the sight of those decorative jumps being taken so magnificently by the horses in such a soaring, magnificent manner that at times they seemed to defy gravity and fly that thrilled her to her soul.

Nathan sat beside her like a statue of himself, hardly moving. She realised, when she was not drawn into the spectacle before her, that he was mentally assessing each rider taking part in the competition. The jumps could be raised or lowered according to the rules of the judges. The poles on the Edinburgh Castle jump were particularly high, and when the first rider, a German called Hans Becke came round to this particular part of the course he urged his horse forward, sending the signals at the right time that made the animal take flight. It cleared the hazard with flying colours, literally, and landed on the other side with an audible thud. This was such a perfect display of horse and man in unison that Lauren, no mean rider herself, would have been hard pushed to see how this feat could be improved upon. She and Nathan were seated near the judges and watched as they gave a high, but not perfect score.

So the day wore on. There was a sense of excitement that only grew as each country came on and took their turn at displaying their horsemanship. The British team were on last - each country had several riders - and it had to be here that disaster struck. The very first rider on a beautiful chestnut mare had another almost faultless round; then came to the fateful Edinburgh leap. There was a sudden bang in another part of the building as the animal approached the fence. It could have been a light bulb popping, or an electrical circuit breaking, but it was such an unexpected sound at a delicate juncture, that it spooked the animal.

It was too late to pull back by then, because if that had been the case the rider, Jason Carter-Manders, would have simply had his horse trot around the arena and come back to the starting point for the jump. Such things were so common the judges would not even have marked him down. But when the sound came the horse had already launched into the air, her ears went back and she lost momentum even though not halting completely, and knocked over the top two poles of the fence, launching her rider into the air so that he fell heavily to the sandy floor of the arena. In the meantime his horse landed awkwardly and fell to one side. It all happened in a bare second, but Nathan was already on his way across the space between them. There was a barrier between the spectators and the main area, but he leapt over this with a breathtaking grace that showed the extent of his physical prowess.

The first thing he did was to attend to the horse, who was thrashing about near the fallen rider. The thing about thoroughbred horses - and Lauren knew this from experience - was that they could panic quite easily, and once panicked could do a lot of damage to themselves, and in this case to those around her. Her admiration for the leap taken by Nathan, that had sent another thrill through her body, was tempered by the fact that he was putting himself in real danger. She too leapt the barrier, perhaps not quite as elegantly as her taller, stronger companion, but with relative ease. It was a matter of seconds before she was at his side and grabbing the reins along with him. This close to the animal she could smell the sweat and desperation of the creature.

'Tsk tsk tsk...,' she cried in her highest voice, knowing that horses responded to such sounds, and a firm grip. Still making soothing sounds, she and Nathan managed to soothe the animal between them and got her to stand up, still trembling. Nathan kept hold of her reins while Lauren turned her attentions to the fallen man. It may have seemed counter intuitive to attend to the horse first, but a horse is a large animal, she had landed near her rider, if she had continued to thrash around she would well have landed on top of the man and injured him badly. Jason was more soiled by his unexpected landing than hurt, as was evidenced by the ripe language with which he expressed his more than wounded feelings as he rose to meet them.

The strange thing was that Lauren had met Jason when she was an up and coming rider in her early years so he warmed to her at once.

'Hellish,' he said.

'Are you all right Jason?' asked Lauren.

'Don't know yet,' he walked up and down a little, 'expect I'm going to have a sore neck and a bit of back strain, and my arms hurt. Too much adrenalin you see, it's keeping me in a state of tension, so I don't really know.' By this time the stewards and first-aiders were on the field. Nathan nodded to the white-coated professionals and handed over the reins of his animal companion, but walked off with them, and continued to soothe her as she walked away. Jason too was led away, much to his chagrin because he wanted to get back on his horse and continue, but he was rambling a little in his speech and Lauren suspected that he might he suffering from what was hopefully a mild concussion. As the horse and her rider were led away the whole audience burst into applause and even a few cheers could be heard, a typical British reaction to good sportsmanship, and Lauren could hardly avoid feeling that some of the good will was for Nathan and what he had done. She did not discount her own contribution either.

Messages came over the sound system informing the gathering that the spectacle would continue. The poles were replaced on the last fence and the spectacle carried on, with the British team coming in a respectable second to the Germans, which was good considering the would-be disaster that had happened.

The show of course did not finish there, and other displays continued including a pony round with children displaying their nascent skills, and a comedy routine including a group of clowns who displayed some exceptional stunt riding that astonished Lauren.

After all this and the main event, it was the end of the day and the pair of them found they were invited to the VIP section. Lauren could sense the reluctance of her companion to take part in these things, and she herself did not want to end up being lectured to about horses by a member of the board, which was what always happened to her at such events, so with as much grace as possible they made their excuses and left.

Chapter Twelve

They went back to his big, black BMW joining the many spectators who were streaming out of the building, people chattering among themselves as they relived the show they had seen earlier. Many of the children were proclaiming how much they wanted a horse or pony, much to the chagrin of some of the hard-pressed parents who knew the expense involved in doing such a thing. Nathan was not amongst those who were yapping their heads off. Instead he opened the door on her side and gestured with a tight smile for her to get inside, and then he went to the other side of the vehicle, got into his own seat and started up the engine.

Lauren could feel the waves of anger and tension coming from him like a tidal wave. Maybe it was a combination of the scents coming from him as she drank in his beautiful male presence. If she closed her eyes she could almost feel as if she was trapped in an enclosed space with magnificent wild beast. She could sense too that he did not want to talk about what had happened, that he was holding it all inside. At the same time she could sense that the anger would erupt at some point like a volcano with pent-up lava that could not be contained suddenly spewing forth. She did not feel in any physical danger but somehow she was afraid of the consequences of such an event.

'I'll take you home,' he said tightly as they drove out of the parking area, the large engine roaring to brutal life as they headed for the ring road that surrounded the capital. 'We'll have to go now. I've got an early rise tomorrow to meet with the arena committee. They'll want their post-mortem on the event.'

'It's a heck of long drive from Edinburgh to Craigton Hill,' said Lauren, 'at least a couple of hours. I know you have your own place in town, that little flat. You'll have to take me home, go to town and drive all the way back to the City the following day.'

'What are you getting at Lauren? I'm not a mind reader.'

'Well you know we could…' she said nothing more but looked at his strong profile and gave a suggestive smile that he saw from the corner of his eye.

'Funnily enough, before we became so friendly I'd already made a reservation with the Grand,' he said, 'I didn't cancel because I wasn't sure if we'd be going to this event together. I was going to call from the car and cancel if we were.' He tapped his fingers on the steering wheel. He was not a man to go on about the obvious. Instead, he headed towards the centre of town. He seemed to know the city like others knew the back of their hands. Soon he was driving towards an overnight parking garage near the city centre. With the BMW steered into a space which he paid for using the credit app on his phone, he emerged from the vehicle, came to her side and opened the door for her.

'I can manage perfectly well,' she protested.

'Yes, well it's a huge car,' he said, 'I've seen grown men stumble as they got out. Just being helpful.' She would not admit the fact even to herself but she felt grateful for his strong arm as she emerged on to the tarmac of the multi-storey. There was a smell of stale sweat, petrol and oil about the place, the air was getting cold after the heat of the day. Her clothes were not much protection from the arid breeze and she shivered a little as the chill seeped in and touched the bare skin of her arms and neck. Of course she had to wear a low-cut dress and a jacket that could not close because of its fashionable cut. She was a sudden victim of her own vanity.

'You're cold,' he said. 'It's a bit of a walk to the hotel, here.' With a gesture that brooked no argument he took off the jacket of his grey, three piece suit and draped it across her shoulders. She was not a small woman, but the jacket was so big it enveloped her like a short coat. The red lining and the thick fabric of the material instantly made her feel a tide of warmth that protected her from the ever-colder atmosphere. The combined scent of his aftershave and natural body odours were also contained in the jacket, sending a shiver through her body, not one of cold this time, but anticipation.

Before leaving the multi-storey car park he clicked a button on his keys and the boot reared upwards with a smooth mechanical hum. He reached in and took out a medium-sized leather case, pressed a button inside the boot and it slid shut with an equally smooth hum. He saw that she was looking at him and indicated the case with his free hand.

'I really did think I was taking you home tonight. I always take a case with all my accoutrements in the back of the car when I'm travelling anywhere, just in case I have a sudden change of plans. I don't have anything for you, I'm afraid.'

'We'll cross that particular bridge when we get to it,' said Lauren, her confidence wilting a little. It had seemed a great idea to do this on the spur of the moment, but now she saw that she was woefully unprepared. Still the feel of his jacket around her was comforting as they made their way down the utilitarian concrete steps of the car park and out to the main street. He carried the suitcase with little effort, as though it was full of feathers.

He strode onwards, his mind on the hotel and his reservation. She had to scurry a little to catch up with him. As he had foretold, they had to walk some distance, but he did not indulge in pointless conversation along the way. She could still sense that anger simmering inside him that the exercise did not dissipate. The Edinburgh Grand was situated in Princes Street not far from the famous Princes Street garden, and the statue of Wojtek the bear, a memorial that somehow marked the Second World War.

The entrance to the Grand was marked by marble pillars ingrained at the top with gold, and semi-circular marble steps down below that lead to a large, black revolving door at which stood a liveried doorman who waited to greet the new couple.

'Couple?' thought Lauren, the word sending a sudden new thrill through her body. Tired though she was from a combination of rising early and working before even coming to Edinburgh, this one word sent a shiver of anticipation through her that enlivened her weary frame.

'I'll have this back,' said Nathan plucking his jacket from her shoulders as they climbed the steps. The hotel was one of the best in Edinburgh, which meant that it was one of the best in Scotland; the first section was a beautiful and spacious reception area. It was not really that late at night – early evening – and when Nathan approached the desk and firmly told the young woman manning the area that he had a reservation she took his name and his details without protest, she barely glanced at Lauren, who gave a faint, nervous chuckle as they began to walk through a spacious hall into the main hotel.

'So you booked a room with a double bed? Wasn't that a bit presumptuous of you? What if I had asked you to drive me all the way home? You would have lost a booking fee.'

'That's where you're wrong,' despite his mood he found time to be faintly amused, 'you have a high estimation of your charms Lauren my love, I always book a double bedroom when I come to this hotel. Not only do I have shares in the business, I'm known for helping arrange a prestigious horse show in the city, so I don't have a room, I have my own suite.' He looked at her with a discerning eye. 'You were working flat out this morning before you came here, weren't you? I've been busy too over the last few days. Do you want a proper meal or would you like to go up and order room service.'

The hotel was quite busy, presumably some of the people here had gone to the very show which he had helped to arrange, and for a moment she had a blissful thought about going upstairs and having just one thing on her personal menu – Nathan. However the practical side of life intervened and she realised that she was indeed feeling hungry. It was as if a roaring lion had come to life inside her at the mention of food.

'That sounds fantastic Nathan, I'm ready if you are,'

'I'm always ready, when you're my size and you're active all the time it's easy to burn off the calories.' That explained some of his moodiness, she thought, he was probably low in blood sugar and needed to top up. She had a sudden naughty thought that he would need his energy later on.

They went into the restaurant which was busy even at that time of night. The maître was standing there with a list in front of him. Other people were standing and waiting to be seated, but when he saw Nathan he gave a big, toothy smile and gestured to him.

'Ah, Meester King, how good to see you again, you wish to be seated with the lady?'

'Hi Luigi,' said Nathan casually but with a flash of humour, 'you haven't returned to menu creation yet?'

'Ah theese is-a-good-a job if you can get it,' said Luigi flashing his whiter than white smile. He darted off and came back a minute later, 'come with me, I get-a you a good table, eet is the best I can do, as we are so busy after thee horse-a show.' He led them to a corner table near a window. That suited Nathan fine, despite his work, Lauren already knew him well enough to realise that he hated being the centre of attention and just liked to get on with his life. From the attention he was getting from staff like Luigi it was obvious that he was well thought of in the Grand.

'I thought you had been away for over three years,' said Lauren as they unfolded their napkins, just as a young waiter appeared.

'For work, yes,' said Nathan, 'but I have been back and forth numerous times for my interests in the market, checking my projects here, and testing the rumours about – well you know,' he paused and for a moment she could see the dark anger rising in him again. Despite having so much, it was obvious that he was a troubled man no matter how he tried to hide his feelings, and her heart went out to him. Before he had a chance to elaborate, the waiter interrupted and they both ordered a main meal only, a hearty beef wellington with all the trimmings. Neither of them was a vegetarian. As the waiter went away Nathan smiled briefly at her.

'You'll have to forgive me, if I have one weakness it's my sweet tooth I will have to indulge and have dessert afterwards.'

'I'll let you into a little secret, so do I, we can both plough on as far as I'm concerned.' It was on her mind to broach the subject of the accident they had witnessed in the arena, but she was sensitive enough to know that the very mention of this would trigger his rising bad mood, and the distraction of dealing with the waiter seemed to have calmed, and relaxed him to an extent. 'Thank you so much for inviting me here,' she said.

'It's a pleasure just to be here with someone like you, a fellow horse person,' he said, 'it's the first time I've been here with a woman too, plenty of businessmen, yes, and the odd friend from the old days, but never anyone as decorous as you.' He spoke the words in an oddly matter-of-fact way, so that he was complimenting her without actually making her feel as if he was picking her out in a singular manner. It was an oddly disquieting way of flattering a female, but as she considered the matter, she realised that she quite liked this way of being the object of his attention.

'I'm glad I'm marginally better than some overweight businessman,' said Lauren with a charming smile.

'Yes you are,' he said, but with a tight smile that showed he was not going to respond whole-heartedly to her joke. The meal came shortly afterwards, and the pair of them dug in quite happily, enjoying their repast in the way that country-bred people tended to do. Lauren was not the slimmest woman on earth, she had curves but also sinews and muscle built up by her job, which still involved a great deal of lifting and handling, and she was in the prime of her womanhood, so she equalled her companion in terms of eating, and neither of them chatted aimlessly during this process, preferring to dine in peace, another throwback to their type of work. At last he sat back and let his fork clatter on the plate as he finished.

'You know when I first met you I thought you were one of those prissy, slight, narcissistic career women, obsessed with self and probably half-starved all the time. Now I see I was mistaken in that assumption,' he said as he wiped his mouth with his napkin. He did not elaborate on his words, but she took the implied compliment for what it was. He was seeing her differently from the well-dressed person he had met at the yard just a few weeks before. Now he could see she was more like him, in essence.

'Have you ever been involved with the 'model' type as I call them?'

'Well, the fact is, you can't be successful in my field without attracting a fair number of followers both male and female,' he said with a faint smile. 'I've been on one or two dates in America, having relationships for perhaps two or three months at a time, but I can't be bothered with their parties, or their faddish little ways, so on the whole, after a short while, we've parted quite amicably.' He looked at the dessert menu, 'time to order.' He opted for a tall ice-cream sundae, while she ordered a banana split.

Truth be told, she was already feeling quite full when the desserts arrived, and as Nathan began eating his with the long spoon provided by the waiter, she found herself looking at the long banana provided. It hadn't been split very well and the ice cream was around it, leaving the fruit on top like some kind of comestible desert island. She picked up the banana with her long, strong fingers, put it to her mouth and began to nibble on it, looking up as she did so to see that Nathan had paused in putting a spoonful of dessert to his mouth and was looking at her.

For some reason this did not embarrass her. She had a sudden, naughty thought of what this must look like to him, and nibbled at the tip of the banana before pausing and putting some of it into her mouth, sucking the fruit as if it was an ice lolly. Only the banana was so soft it began to disintegrate straight away, so still holding it in her hand, she swallowed the pulp. She fed more of the fruit in her mouth, sucked again and swallowed once more, continuing the process until the whole of the banana was gone. During this process, which took barely a minute, although it seemed much longer, Nathan resumed his ice cream sundae, but did not take his eyes off her the whole time. He laid down his long spoon as he finished and raised his thick, black arched eyebrows at her but said nothing.

Chapter Thirteen

As if powered by an invisible motor between them, the pair pushed away their dessert dishes. Lauren hadn't bothered finishing hers. He tipped the waiter on the way out, with many thanks, and the pair of them went out of the elegant restaurant and headed up the wide, curving staircase that led to their room. She didn't have the vaguest clue about the room number since it was Nathan who had collected the key card from reception. On the way out of the restaurant Nathan collected the bottle of champagne he had ordered to go with their repast, carrying the bottle in one hand and two fluted glasses in the other. He handed these to Lauren as he halted before room number twenty-four, passing the card through the magnetic strip so that it triggered the lock, He pushed the door open with one strong hand and gestured for her to go inside with the other. As she walked inside Lauren put a suggestive wiggle into her walk, well aware that he would be looking at her bottom. Though she tried to avoid the thought that came to her mind, she was well aware that she possessed a pair of shapely buttocks, and that these were enhanced by the dress she had chosen to wear.

The suite was beautiful in structure, with a living room style area that led directly into a large bedroom. The room was equipped with easy chairs and large, glass-topped coffee table. Nathan sat the champagne on the table and poured two glasses of bubbly, while Lauren took a peek into the bedroom, which was laid out in colours of pink and gold, with an en suite bathroom. The bed was large, and decorated with a floral pillows, and a duvet, one corner of which had been pulled back to reveal the crisp white sheets beneath. She could have had all the men she wanted over the years, could have been in this situation many times, but she was glad that she had waited for someone like Nathan, a man so masculine even the hairs on her neck prickled when she was near him.

She went back through, picked up her glass and saluted him. 'To you and your wonderful horse show Nathan.' He drank with her. She felt the delicious bubbles dance on her tongue, tickle the inside of her nose, and swallowed half of her wine in one smooth gulp. It was wonderfully liberating to be here and doing these things, freed from the worries of her day-to-day existence at Craigton, and even better to be with a handsome man like Nathan.

But it was as if her salutation was a lit fuse to a bomb. He too drank deeply, draining his glass. He had sallow skin anyway and a deep tan as a result of spending so much time outdoors, but now his face was as black as a thunderous sky, his brows descending towards the frown lines between his eyes.

'It's not good enough,' he said almost in agony. Lauren got up and went to him. It was as if she was in the room with some huge wounded animal, she could feel the waves of fear and anguish rolling off him like a tide. She tried to touch him on one knotted shoulder but he shrugged her off like a feather and strode around the large room. His agitation was obvious.

'My first big show…a disaster.' Lauren decided the best way to deal with this was to sit down and not try to halt his progress. From dealing with horses she knew that the best way to deal with an agitated animal was to give it space to work off excess energy. As far as she was concerned men were no different to other males, they didn't speak, about their problems, they acted. She knew it was not a fashionable view to hold, but men and women were distinct in how they dealt with things.

'What is it?' she asked, knowing full well.

'Dogged by bad luck, how could I let this happen again?' he was not so much taking to her as to thin air. In some ways it was as if she wasn't there. He was venting his anger.

'You did your best,' said Lauren.

'Well my best wasn't good enough,' said Nathan as if suddenly becoming aware of her presence. 'Not good enough at all. He could have been killed, broken his neck or the horse could have trampled him.' He focussed on Lauren. 'I'm sorry, I'm not good company. That moment when the fence came down, it's on my mind. It's all right, you take the bed, I'll sleep in one of the armchairs. I've slept in far worst places.' Lauren stood up again. He was still pacing back and forth but she did not come too close.

'You'll do no such thing. Also I won't have you blaming yourself any longer for what happened. There was a bang somewhere, a horse was startled and knocked over a few poles, and a rider fell. The trouble with you is that your mind is going back to a life-altering disaster.'

'It's a repeat of the same thing, they won't trust me again.' Lauren stood in front of him, hands on her hips. As the boss of a large riding stable and jump manager herself, she was used to dealing with recalcitrant stable lads and lasses, tempered by the fact that she was quite willing to muck in with regard to her own business. She wasn't about to miss and hit the wall.

'Listen to me Mister. I was riding Jewel down to the Meadows just after taking over the business. I was a bit rusty because I'd been away for a few years, and not to put too fine a point on it, I fell off and hit the ground with a thud. It hurt, and I was lucky I got away with a few bruises. For a week I avoided riding her altogether, fearing that the worse had happened, and that all I could do in the future was deal with paperwork. Then one day Yasmin asked me why I hadn't been out for a hack for a while and I realised that quite frankly I was suffering from fear. I went into that stable, saddled Jewel, took her out and went for another ride, quivering with anguish the whole time.'

'That has no bearing on what happened,' said Nathan, pausing and staring at the fierce creature she had turned into as if seeing her for the first time.

'That's where you're wrong,' said Lauren. 'What happened out there could have happened at any time, at any show. Can I ask you, did you run the jump design past the committee?'

'You know that sounds like a stupid question? Of course I did, there wouldn't have been a course otherwise. In fact they suggested several themes and once or twice they actually asked me to increase the levels of risk.' Lauren did not say anything for several seconds and watched as the thought began to dawn on her companion. 'They hired me because they knew I had been designing some pretty spectacular courses in America. Maybe one or two even knew my history, but they didn't care.' Lauren remained silent, crossing her arms across her chest and watching him with a half smile on her pretty face. 'We actually saved a tricky situation didn't we?' Finally she broke her silence.

'You didn't seem to understand that what happened today would never have been thought of as your fault. It's because the event took you back to a similar situation all those years ago, when a fence of your design failed catastrophically, leading to the death of that beautiful animal, Buck, and the serious injury of his rider. It's like comparing apples and pears, the two things can't be compared with each other. Besides, I have to say that the way you vaulted that fence and went to still that horse, why, it aroused something in my maidenly bosom that I haven't felt for a while.' She knew that she was starting to tease now, to distract him from the vagaries of his own mind. Quite simply he was suffering from a deep-seated guilt that had been brought out by the events of the day.

'Lane Marsh,' he said, 'he was my assistant. He vanished the evening before the Dumfries event. He did it, I know he did, but it was 'only' a horse, not a murder. I couldn't charge him. I...I...'

From her viewpoint it was as if she was watching the plug being taken out of a vat full of simmering acid. Suddenly all the bile inside Nathan drained away. He sat down heavily in one of the armchairs, put his hands to his face, and wept for a good fifteen seconds, hearty male sobs that showed how deeply he had held everything inside. Lauren curbed her instinct to go to his side and comfort him, knowing that this was a deeply private matter, that in some way he had even forgotten there was another person present. Finally he stopped and looked at the ground for a while then got up.

'I guess you think I'm weak for that,' he said in a voice that brooked no other viewpoint, his face looking bleak. He began to open the door.

'Where are you going?'

'I'll see if they have a spare room so I can leave you in peace.' She had a sudden picture of him lying in an annexe smaller than his bedroom at home, brooding all the way through the night. It seemed that the events of three years ago had affected him a lot more deeply than he had cared to admit even to himself. Lauren once more showed that strong side that seemed so at odds with her femininity – from a male point of view that was. To her strong women were the norm, and she was going to show this dominant male that side of her as long as she needed to.

'You'll stay right here mister. So, you showed a few emotions, it's been a heck of a long day for you, you've been keyed up the whole time waiting for something to happen, and when it did, you rose to the occasion magnificently, no-one could have asked for a better response, you got there a full thirty seconds before the stewards and that half minute was enough to avert a hugely dangerous situation. You'll come in right now and get to your bed, you must be exhausted, and as for sleeping in a chair – if I have to, that's what I'll do. You're the man of the hour.' He had already presented the key card and the door was half open, but now he turned to her and closed it again. The words were pulled out of him like teeth at the dentist.

'You – you don't think any the less of me for what happened?'

'Nathan, you don't understand, you're seeing it through the lens of that awful event three years ago that changed your life, but now you're a hero, to me and possibly to hundreds who attended the show.' She was wrong in one way in her trite assessment, but that was for the future. 'Now it's time to lighten up. Did you enjoy your meal?'

'I suppose so,' Nathan blinked at the sudden change of subject. She was walking towards him in a womanly manner as she spoke, wiggling her hips and shaking her bosom a little.

Chapter Fourteen

'Has your meal made you a little sleepy?' As she spoke she drew closer to him, 'because if it has, I suggest that it might be time for bed.' It was not hard to convey her message to him. He looked like a man who has been chained up, but who has thrown off the shackles of his imprisonment. In almost a dreamlike state he turned and wrapped his strong, muscular arms around her. There was no doubt about her feelings for him, as he aroused in her emotions that she had not experienced for a long time. The thing was, she knew from the events on her land, Craigton that he had the same feelings for her, only they had been suppressed by the tension of preparing for the show and the events of the day.

Releasing some of his pent-up emotions seemed to have done him some good. Even as he embraced her and she bathed in his different scents – why even the shampoo he used to wash his hair in the shower had a gorgeous smell – intermingled with the smell of his aftershave and his natural body odours, she felt even more as if her whole body was alive to his touch. If she wasn't careful she would experience the act right there and then. He pulled away from her and as if by some silent accord the pair of them walked into the bedroom, somehow savouring the silence between them, except for the fact that his breathing was somehow rougher, harsher than before, showing that he was becoming aroused by her presence.

Like all men he was not one for words at a time like this, she turned and took off her purple jacket, putting it on the bedroom chair, then her fancy lace gloves that she had been carrying, and pulled her dress over her head so that she was standing in front of him in her lacy underwear. She was aware that he wasn't just looking at her; he was drinking in her presence like a man who has been thirsty for too long and is in need of slaking his thirst. She was aware that her underwear was ridiculously sheer, and wondered why had she chosen it so long ago in the morning when she was getting ready to go? The only thing she could think of was the fact that she knew she was going to be with him all day, and that at some point they might be doing this particular thing.

Nathan was not slow off the mark, as she stripped down to her underwear he took off his own clothes, but instead of leaving them on the floor, like most men, he went back through and sat them on one of the living room armchairs, walking back through in only his blue silk boxer shorts. It was clear that from the tent in the front of his underpants that he was excited in a primal fashion by her near-naked presence.

She came forward and embraced Nathan again. The rooms were not overly warm, but it had been a hot day and when she shivered, it was not with cold but excitement, the excitement of being here with the man she had been waiting for. She began to unhook her bra, but he shook his head, putting out his strong arms and suddenly pushing down on top of her head, an indication of what he wanted, and what she was more than willing to give.

She knelt before him on the soft carpet made of proper thick wool – there would be no nylon burns here – and pulled down his boxer shorts, seeing his stiff cock spring into view. She didn't have that much experience with the male organ, but even in her experience she could see that his cock was a good size, so big that she had to hold it with both hands as she guided it to her willing mouth.

She noticed that he was not circumcised and rubbed his foreskin back and forth as she engulfed the head of his cock, wrapping her red lips around it as it entered her mouth. She began sucking furiously on his salty cock, but not passively, moving her head back and forward on his glans penis to stimulate him to the highest degree with her mouth, still holding his cock with one hand as she did so. The other hand had snaked round and she was holding one of his muscular buttocks as she worked up a pumping action with her other hand and her mouth.

He groaned aloud, and buried his fingers in her hair, tugging gently at her fair locks as she performed these actions and partially thrusting forward, showing that he was more than enjoying her attentions. She sucked his cock for what seemed like a long time, but he pulled back and spoke in a voice thick with emotion.

'I want to see you Lauren, see you and take you.' She was not averse to this request because she was already aware that her pussy was soaking wet, ready for him in the most obvious way. She pulled back from his cock, gave it a lingering stroke with her long fingers, and unhooked her bra. Her breasts sagged a little as she did this, and for a second she regretted her fuller figure, a regret that did not linger when she saw how hungrily he was looking at her. She was aware that her nipples were hard, even harder than they became when she played with herself in her lonely bed at night. She pulled down her panties and stepped out of them. She was not one of those women who shaved down there, and knew he was looking at her pussy hair with fascination. Slowly he walked forward, his cock straining stiffly as he did so.

Lauren was only dimly aware that the bed was somewhere behind her, which was unusual for her because she was normally hyper-aware of her surroundings. There was a sort of delicious fuzziness in her head, a cloud of dual consciousness that was somehow engulfing the pair of them, her with this beautiful man, and what he was about to do with her. Her bare legs contacted the softness of the bed, and she let herself go, falling backwards on to the ultra-soft duvet as she did so. She was aware of her breasts falling to either side as lay down, and put her hands on each side of her breasts, pulling them together and pointing her nipples ceiling wards, well aware that Nathan was advancing onwards at a relentless pace.

He paused in front of her and looked at her lower parts, her legs spread to expose everything to him.

'We have to stop,' he said harshly, regretfully, 'I don't have a condom, I wasn't planning for this to happen, and this has to stop now.'

'No, it's all right,' breathed Lauren, 'I'm taking the pill. It has nothing to do with sex Nathan, I was having irregular – well you know, so the doctor advised me to take them to regulate me. You're safe, you can go on.'

'If you're sure, because I can come on those wonderful tits,' he said, his cock still straining forward as he spoke. She pushed her breasts together again, her nipples stiffening even further at his words, if possible.

'No, no, I want you,' she said, 'put it in me, put it in me now you magnificent beast.' But it was not to be, not at that moment. It was obvious that he wanted to push his organ home, to invade her wet pussy, but he seemed to be a fair-minded man in some ways. She had pleasured his cock with her mouth so it was his turn to return the favour. He went down on his knees and brought his mouth to her pussy.

Suddenly this was what she wanted him to do, even though it was something that she had never experienced before. She took her hands away from her breasts and put them into his thick, soft hair, Once more the scent of his shampoo came to her, a delicious citrus scent that mixed with that of his own body odours and hers.

He put his hands on the outside of her thighs and held her warm flesh as he went forward to her pussy. She could not see what he was doing because his head obscured her view, but she could certainly *feel* what he was doing. He put out his tongue and found her clitoris, that little nub of pleasure that she had often played with in the night as she thought wistfully of a man who could be doing the same thing for her. She had no need to be wistful now, because the most beautiful man she had known was pleasuring her in the most intimate manner possible. In some ways it was more intimate than actual sex.

The thing was, it could have been a horrible experience if he had not known what he was doing, because he could have been too rough or could have missed the target altogether. But Nathan knew exactly what he was doing and his long, agile tongue flicked her clitoris almost with a kind of joyous glee, like a sprite dancing over a sparkling stream. She threw her head back, pushing down on his coarse black hair, as waves of pleasure went through her body. This was the real thing and it was good. Good? It was better than good; it was the best experience she'd ever had with a man, as far from the school boyish fumbling she had experienced with others as it could be.

Finally, after a minute or two to licking her clit, he stood up and put his hands on her breasts. He was so tall and strong, a real man, big, solid and muscular. He reminded her of one of his own horses, a big solid brute full of force and energy. He bent forward and softly licked her nipples in turn. Well it would have been difficult to suck them both at the same time; although in a calmer moment he might have tried.

As she lay there he managed to pull down one of the pillows, and thrust it behind her head to support her neck so that she was more comfortable. They were still not in the traditional bed position, her legs were still hanging off, but he put his strong hands on either side of her, grabbed her buttocks and pushed her back so that she was more on the bed than before. She lifted her legs and spread them apart. Her head being in a better position she was able to watch as his hard cock came forward to her entrance. She could not believe how well he had lasted. In her limited experience, after a good cock sucking, and licking a clit, most men would have exploded by now, but it seemed even in the midst of sexual excitement he was in control.

His cock was now at her entrance, so she bucked forward with her hips to try and get his cock to impale her, her vaginal juices flowing so much she feared she would leave a stain on the floral duvet.

Then the head of his penis was in her. Such was the size of his cock he did not try to push into her in one go, instead he put in the tip of his cock and worked it back and forth, widening her entrance and moistening his cock with her juices until he was wet enough to go in deeper.

And he did go deeper.

He pushed into her gradually, building up a good rhythm so that he was thrusting into her in a forceful and pleasing manner until finally his cock was filling up her willing vagina. This was the way sex should be.

Lauren was not just a passive recipient of his massive cock; she moved her hips in unison with his thrusting movements so that he would have the maximum impact on her willing body. In her (admittedly limited) experience she knew that men did not last long before they were spent, but she told herself that she didn't care, that the sensation of him being inside her was enough, that she was experiencing more than she had ever dreamed of before, and if he came then she would still have had the most wonderful experience. She was not disappointed in what he was doing, but as he built up the rhythm of his thrusts in time with the movement of her hips, he licked and sucked her nipples alternately, holding her ample breasts in his hands as he did so, and with such obvious lust that it turned her on even more.

The scent of him was almost overpowering too as she breathed in, instead of just his aftershave or the smell of his shampoo, he was giving off a musky male odour that seemed to somehow cloy in her nostrils, filtering through her entire being. She wasn't just experiencing the force of his body; she was becoming part of him.

He was becoming part of her. There was a sweet scent that came from her own body too, a mixture of her juices down below as he thrust in and out of her, and of her own perspiration, that began to build up on her skin as their frenetic love-making continued. He surely couldn't last much longer, she thought as he kept thrusting into her, going deeper and harder than she might have thought possible. Once more she buried her fingers in his thick, dark hair and pulled at his head, pushing him back down to her breasts.

The feeling building up in her was one of wanting to explode, so dynamic were the thrusting movements of his powerful thighs as he pumped his cock in an out of her, his body pushing into hers so powerfully that she was actually being pushed further up on to the bed, more fully on to the duvet.

'Oh, oh, oh,' she cried as he continued his powerful movements, her hands clutching so powerfully to his head that she must be straining his neck, and she had powerful hands and arms from being a horsewoman for so long. As she felt him shudder with the depth of the powerful waves of excitement that were going through his body, her own tremors were too much to contain, and she felt a surge of sexual ecstasy pass through her body that she had never experienced before in her life. She was aware they were experiencing a simultaneous climax, also something that she had never known before in her short life. For a few seconds, so powerful was the experience that she actually blacked out. She came back and saw that he was still above her, his powerful arms preventing his large body from crushing hers.

She could feel his cock rapidly shrinking inside her and had the presence of mind to reach over to the bedside cabinet on which the hotel had thoughtfully sat a box of lavender-tinted tissues, grab a bunch of them and put these between her legs, and above the duvet as he withdrew. She could feel a mixture of his and her juices trickling down between her legs, and was glad she'd had the presence of mind to contain them.

'Oh Nathan, that was wonderful,' she said, 'I love you.' She regretted the words as soon as she said them.

He gave her a dark, almost angry look, rose and went into the en suite toilet, where she heard the sound of him peeing, and then the splash as the shower was switched on. It didn't surprise her that he had left that way since he was a man of few words, and his climax must have left him wondering what the hell he was doing with this woman he barely knew.

She felt like crawling under the duvet and nestling there but instead she got to her feet and went into the bathroom. As befitted a hotel like this there was a heated towel rack in the corner complete with huge, fluffy cream-coloured towels also with embroidered roses on them, the hotel seemed to have a thing about roses. But her attention was caught by the large beautiful male standing there.

Now that she was looking at him naked, it was obvious that the slimness of his waist and the breadth of his shoulders was not an illusion caused by the tailored suits he liked to wear. His washboard stomach and the muscles on his arms and legs indicated that here was a man who enjoyed attending the gym at least three times a week.

He gave her a less severe look as she entered.

'That was good,' he said, 'you're a beautiful woman, it's been a long time since I've made love to anybody, what with the demands of the job.' He looked her over uncritically and she realised that she was enjoying his gaze. There was no doubt about it that any embarrassment had been quickly swept away by their lustful encounter.

He jerked his head towards the corner where the shower was splashing so invitingly. He did not have to say anything, so clear was the gesture. They had a great deal more fun together, and then it was time for bed.

Chapter Fifteen

Lauren walked about the beautiful department store in the centre of Edinburgh. It was still quite early. She was wearing the clothes from the race day. She was far from extravagant; the problems with the riding school, and the need to pay her staff had stopped her from buying as many clothes as she wanted over the years. She saw a lovely two-piece outfit, skirt and jacket, in a nice powder blue shade that she knew would suit her fair complexion.

She walked about quite soberly wondering if her expression showed that she was deliriously happy, her head up in the clouds, her mind in a half-daze as thoughts of Nathan kept intruding into the more prosaic act of shopping. She was alone because she was determined to find an outfit that would allow her to grace his meeting with the event management board.

This morning had been leisurely. They had both awoken early. Twice during the night they had made love, far more gently and less frantically than the night before. They had ordered room service eating heartily from a large selection of breakfast fare including toast and creamy highland butter, cereal and croissants. He was a big man and she had used up so much energy that she needed the calories to bring her back to full physical perfection.

He was going to leave her in the hotel while he attended the meeting later that day, but she insisted that she would be going with him. He had pointed out that the meeting would be boring, but Lauren was far from put off by this. She wanted to see how the industry really worked, having been part of the equestrian scene for years.

It was obvious that he was flattered by her interest in the business and not just his body. But that was why she was here, in this very store. She didn't want to turn up in the same outfit, which would make it obvious that the pair of them had spent the night together. She very much wanted to show up as a business woman in her own right.

Lauren tried to tell herself that she really needed to do this, but it would mean a few weeks if not months of scrimping and saving. The thought troubled her a little, but she felt that changing was the right thing to do, after all she had volunteered for this trip, and she couldn't put her financial issues on to her new lover. Lover! The word sent a delicious tingle down her spine.

She was approaching the counter with the new clothes and various feminine accoutrements when she saw a tall, well-dressed individual come in through the door. Her heart skipped a few beats, another cliché that was true, when she saw it was Nathan.

'I thought I would find you here,' he said.

'Hello you,' said Lauren with a beaming smile. 'I'll just pay for this then we'll go back to the hotel.'

'We'll go back to the hotel,' he said, 'but you're not paying for this.'

'Excuse me?' she swiftly lost her smile.

'You say you need to dress the part, which is fair enough, but I'm the one responsible for you being here. You'll add this to my expense account.'

'I don't take my business needs from another person,' she said proudly. 'I'll pay for my own outfit.'

'Fair enough,' he shrugged his broad shoulders. 'But you would be a fool not to take advantage of my arrangements.'

'What do you mean?'

'All my assets are part of the business. I don't receive a wage, everything I do is part of business expenses, the suits the car, everything, and because it's all part of my expenses I can claim back VAT on everything. I get paid a dividend if the business is doing well, and I get nothing if it isn't.'

'You don't earn a wage?' It seemed a strange arrangement to her.

'Yep. Well, Lauren, when was the last time you got paid? In fact don't answer that, I know how much it has cost you to keep the stables running. There's a saying that business expenses walk on two legs, well in your case, they walk on four, I don't deal with our four-legged friends directly, I just make the courses, but I know the breeders and the stock managers and the countless equine centres and I know what it takes.'

'So, in fact you're saying that if you pay for this outfit you can claim the money back through the business?' confirmed Lauren.

'Exactly, and as my associate, with whom I hope to partner for a new design testing centre, I think I'm justified in doing this.' They approached the counter together; he produced a platinum coloured business card and paid as the assistant rang up the goods. He took the receipt as it was rung up and tucked this into his wallet.

'Need this for the tax man,' he said. Lauren followed him out of the store with mixed feelings. She still had the nagging feeling that she had allowed a man to impose his strong feelings about buying her a present on to her. Yet his logic was impeccable. He was charging everything to the business and wouldn't lose any personal money.

Back at the hotel, he looked at her as she emerged from the bathroom wearing the outfit. In her preparations she had also washed, dried, and brushed her fair hair so that it hung down well. The outfit accentuated her shapely figure. He was sitting in an armchair wearing his dark grey suit, with a sober blue tie.

'Well, well,' said Nathan, 'you clearly scrub up well my love; you'll certainly make a change at this meeting. I was looking forward to being thoroughly bored, but you'll stir up a few of those old fuddy-duddies, and at least make the day a little bit more entertaining.'

'What about the points I might have to make?' asked Lauren. 'I might have a few worthwhile things to say.' He gave a grin that suddenly made him look a great deal more boyish.

'You think so? I'm counting on it Lauren. You don't think I'm taking you along for arm candy do you?'

'I hope not,' she said with dignity, a little annoyed that he seemed to be making fun of her, then laughing inwardly at her own reaction. They left the hotel together, a beautiful couple, and walked to his waiting car.

Chapter Sixteen

They were driving back to Craigton late that afternoon, and would be home by later in the evening. As he had predicted, her presence at the meeting had caused a mild stir. Most of those attending were senior members of the equine board as befitted such an august organisation, so amongst those elders she was like a fresh young rose in a field of withered flowers, easily the youngest there. It was not just a matter of being there, she actually held forth about one or two matters to do with the national organisation that made sense and actually contributed to the debate.

She couldn't always concentrate though, not sitting there with Nathan, who in his fresh suit, crisp white shirt, new tie, and his hair freshly washed, still wearing that gorgeous aftershave, was easily the centre of attention. Once or twice she caught one or two of the older ladies looking at her in a way that could be easily construed as envy.

Then it came to the matter of the fall.

'I don't normally apologise,' said Nathan, 'but I feel perhaps I should have gone over the design of the Edinburgh Castle fence one more time before the actual show. However I did my best to mitigate the situation. That's all I can say in my own defence.'

Mr McKinstry, the chairman of the board, looked thoughtfully at their design protégé.

'My dear young man, haven't you seen the morning papers?' Nathan could hardly say that he had been too busy making love to Lauren that morning to see anything of the sort, but she had the grace to lower her head, staring at the table and blushing a little. The chairman produced a copy of the 'Edinburgh News,' opened at the third page. There, large as life and twice as handsome, was a picture of Nathan leaping over the barrier looking like some big vigorous animal in action. This was followed by supplementary pictures below showing him reining in the skittish horse while Lauren was shown with her arm around Jason, the rider.

'Horse-show hero saves the day!' was the headline above the picture. There wasn't much content to the article, which was a couple of paragraphs in the corner, but they did point out that Nathan and his mysterious female friend had saved what could have been a disastrous situation.

'My dear fellow,' said McKinstry, 'we have here one of the biggest adverts for the equine arts that I have ever seen in my life. This isn't the only article you know, you made the National dailies too, and there was an article about you on morning television. You've done the National Equine League a massive favour.'

When the pair of them left the meeting it was clear that he was not in a good mood. 'I was going to go back to the hotel,' he said, 'but that's not going to happen. I'll ask them to pack any of my stuff and pay the extra. I'll collect it another day.'

'Why would you do that?' asked Lauren.

'Because where there's that kind of headline there will be reporters. I'm surprised they haven't tracked us down already, I suppose it's because I didn't tell anyone where we would be staying.'

'Are you going home then?' He looked at the clock on the dashboard.

'It's getting towards the end of the afternoon, it's been a long day and we haven't had any lunch. I know a little place we can go for dinner if you're hungry, it's a little early.'

'That's fine,' said Lauren, but it was clear that she was feeling a little disappointed. He did not say anything, but she knew that one thought had been in both of their minds. After the meeting they could have gone back to the hotel and made love before returning home. It seemed that the same thoughts were going through his head; the atmosphere inside the SUV was almost palpable. He drove for about twenty minutes. Edinburgh is not a large city and this brought them to the outskirts of the capital, and he drew into a large car park which was fairly deserted, a couple of hundred yards from what could only be described as a rural inn, an ancient, low building with a thatched roof.

'This is the Lothian Inn,' he said, 'they do the most delicious beef and ale pies I've ever tasted. I brought a change of clothes so I don't splash my good shirt and tie when I dig in, these clothes are expensive I can't risk marking them in any way; I was planning to bring us here later, after – well after the hotel.' The back windows of the SUV were heavily tinted. He pressed a button and extraordinarily, the front windows also developed a tint, although not as heavy.

'It's not the first time I've had to use this thing as a travelling bedroom,' said Nathan.

'How could you do that?' asked Lauren. He glanced at her briefly without answering, stepped out of the car and went into his case in the boot, fetching out a couple of loose sweaters. She was still in her new outfit, so he looked at her thoughtfully.

'One of these would do for you, you're quite tall and you have a long back. If you tuck it in you'll be fine.' It took her only seconds to cotton on to what he was doing.

'This has nothing to do with stains on a tie or a blouse; you're making sure we change our appearance in case the press somehow manage to track us down. You're paranoid sonny boy.' He grinned at her.

'Am I that transparent? Well you're too smart for your own good missy. The truth is, I know that they'll try to feature me as some kind of hero, and then they'll track down the fact that I previously changed my name, left the country and built up the business from scratch. If I avoid them this will be a one-day wonder then I'll be completely forgotten.' Lauren had to admit to herself that it was a good idea. She knew that publicity could go either way, despite some people saying that it could never be bad. She remembered the story of a man who manufactured cheap jewellery, and who appeared on a chat show and branded his own product 'crap,' shortly afterwards his business went down the tubes and he lost it all. They got back into the spacious vehicle.

'Besides, I haven't answered your question,' he said, grinning again in that school-boy manner, pleased to show off a new trick. He pressed a couple of buttons on what was effectively a technological wonder of a control panel compared to that on her own car. There was a buzzing noise, and as Lauren turned and looked the back seats seemed to retreat like magic. 'The boot isn't too full; the case is at the front. The seats automatically go backwards and fold into themselves. Keep sitting upright, press forwards a little.'

Lauren obeyed the instruction and felt rather than saw the back of her own seat vanish as it folded into the space vacated by the back ones.

'This is fantastic,' she said, because they were now in a space that could only be described as roomy compared with what it had been before. Also, because it was cushioned it was ultra-comfortable.

'All I need to do is remember my mummy sleeping bag, and a pillow, and I have a home from home,' he said. 'I've parked in various areas, and I just use public toilets nearby or bushes and tree shelter if I'm in the wild. It means I can be away for days at a time. It's paid for itself in hotel prices several times over.' Lauren smiled at him, and a sudden, naughty thought came into her head. She reached forward and kissed him on the lips, a kiss that he returned, but with some surprise in his manner at the unexpected nature of her approach. She pulled back and smiled at him. 'Of course I have to protect my new outfit,' she said, taking off her new jacket and putting it to one side, then unbuttoning her fresh blouse, aligning it with her jacket. He looked at her ample breasts in the daylight that filtered through the tinted windows. He did not say anything but carefully took off his suit jacket, undid his tie, and took off his own shirt and trousers, kneeling in front of her wearing only his boxer shorts and long, black socks.

By this time Lauren was down to her lacy panties, her breasts jiggling as she leaned forward and into his strong, manly embrace. They kissed fervently. There was something about the richness of the summer day, and not to put too fine a point on it, the fresh air that trickled through the ventilation system and into the car, that made her tingle all over. The two of them were aroused in a way that they hadn't been in the hotel. It may have been the thought of where they were, and the danger of discovery, but Lauren felt almost dizzy with desire. This was not just being sexual with a man for whom she was falling fast; it was also, it was a dangerous, edgy act, a defiance of the norms of society. The danger of being discovered added some piquancy to the sexual nature of what they were doing.

She thought her nipples had been stiff in the hotel, but now it felt as if they were going to burst as her pussy throbbed with desire. They kissed for a while longer and she did not resist when he put his tongue in her mouth. They locked their mouths for more a while, then they parted and he paid attention to her breasts as they still knelt in front of each other. He held a pendulous breast in each hand, and kneaded the flesh a little as he sucked each nipple in turn. She moaned aloud as he tongued her nipples and pressed down on the top of his head as he did so, enjoying the sensation as he licked, sucked and very gently nibbled her nipples. She gave one particularly loud moan and realised once more where she was, that if anyone else came into the car park they might hear her. It was not an unpleasant sensation.

It was obvious that they were not going to spend as much time doing this as they might have done at the hotel. She pulled down his boxer shorts and his cock sprang forth. He kicked off the shorts as she sprawled backwards on the cushioning of the well-padded leather seats. She did not remove her lacy panties as she fell back, but instead pulled them to one side exposing the lips of her vagina.

This time the need was more urgent, caused as much by their circumstances as by lust, and he took the invitation as it was and penetrated her there and then. He thrust into her so powerfully that she slid along the leather of the seat and nearly bumped her head on the frame of the vehicle. She put out her arms and braced herself, her ample breasts bouncing as he thrust into her time and time again.

This time around, his love making was just as vigorous as it had been in the hotel. He pushed into her time and time again as she yielded to his male eagerness, her buttocks warming on the leather as he made love to her in a way she had experienced with no other man.

The one thing she hadn't realised was that the both of them were not silent partners in the joint endeavour they called love making. It started with her moans as she allowed him to put his cock into her. The size of it delighted her, and she gave out a few involuntary moans as he entered her. Then, as he continued to thrust, she was aware that she was giving vent to a series of gasps a and moans that she could not help, although as soon as she noticed these she tried to lower the sound, aware of what it would be like to stand outside the BMW and hear what was going on.

Even so, she was unable to stop herself from saying things like : 'Yes, yes, YES!' as he pounded his cock into her, letting go of the bulkhead, reaching out her hands and grasping his muscular buttocks as if trying to pull all of him inside her. This, along with squeals and moans as he continued to fuck her made this anything but a silent event.

He too was not without his noisy side. As he continued to push back and forth in a wonderful rhythm that built up into a symphony of sex, he too made moaning and groaning noises that chimed with her own, only they were on a much lower register so that at times he even seemed to be growling at her in the depths of his passion.

'I wanna give it to you, give it to you all day long,' he said at one point, 'because you're the one who turns me on. I could do it to you all day and all night too. That's what I want, that's what I want from you, you sexy thing.'

The noises around them were compounded by the fact that the BMW, like all cars, was an object that sat on springs. It was swaying back and forth in a regular rhythm with their bodies, even making a few creaking sounds, which added rather than detracting from their lovemaking. The leather too had a rich, somewhat musky smell that tied in with his and her own scents. He had an air freshener in the car too, which had an aroma of fresh pine that somehow mingled with the rest and somehow made the experience even richer.

It was as if she was fully alive for the first time. There was only one other manner in which she had experienced such a rich mixture of physical experiences, and she did not want to admit this even to herself, but it was when she was out horse riding. The feel of a mighty animal between her legs, the rushing of the wind as she got her steed to canter then gallop faster and faster, the scents of summer that assaulted her nostrils at that speed, the feeling of being on a timeless journey, they were all there.

Then it was all over. He seemed to have that special knack of getting them to climax together, another thing she had never experienced with another man. Not that she had known that many men in her life, just that the ones she had experienced were not as good as this one. The pair of them lay together in contented silence for a few minutes, and then he gave a groan and pulled out of her. Once more he showed her how prudent he was by pulling a packet of tissues from the side pocket of the door, so that their juices could be caught before they stained the seats of the car.

'These are awfully handy,' said Lauren 'seems to me you've done this kind of thing before.' For a moment she found herself jealous of the phantom women who might have done the very same thing in the BMW. He gave a merry laugh as he lay back and pulled his trousers back on.

'Believe you me, you're the first. The only reason I have tissues is because when you're eating a carry-out meal in a car it can get pretty messy, and I want to keep this thing in good condition. Besides, I only got it when I came back at the end of last year and I've been too busy running up and down the country to do anything else but sleep and eat in here.' Lauren warmed to him at these words. She had been the first for him in here, which showed that he wanted her only.

'I just hope when we get to this inn no-one's talking because the car was rocking,' said Lauren as she donned her bra and pulled on the long sleeved purple t-shirt her lover supplied for her.

'It's all right; I parked as far away from the building as possible, under the shadow of a tree. It's unlikely anybody noticed anything, and if they did, well, they'll just be jealous.'

She had put her fair hair up with bright red clips when they were at the business meeting, but now she let it down so that it flowed around her shoulders. She had put on her red skirt, while in his t-shirt and black trousers, his hair flattened down, wearing his reading glasses, he looked very far from the astute businessman she had seen earlier that day.

Chapter Seventeen

They went demurely into the olde worlde atmosphere of the inn. It was a place of low ceilings, rustic bare wood, roughly carved wooden chairs and scrubbed tables made of cedar wood. They went to the back of the pub and ordered an early dinner from a girl who looked about fifteen years old but who was probably about twenty. Naturally they ordered the steak and ale pie with all the trimmings. Lauren also decided to order an ice cream dessert. There was one thing about having a lot of vigorous sex, it burnt up the calories like nobody's business, especially as they had skimped on lunch. They were mid-way through their tasty repast when the door of the inn opened and a stranger came in who was dressed in a shirt and tie along with jeans, and who carried a phone and an old-fashioned notebook. An SLR camera dangled around his neck. The stranger ordered a soft drink at the bar and looked around the pub, his gaze resting on the various couples and families who were dining there.

Lauren decided to act as if she was completely untroubled, and ate with her long hair hanging down in an untidy manner which was most unlike her, while Nathan concentrated on tucking into his mashed potatoes, paused and yawned for a second, burped and went back to his meal. It was as good as a disguise. Lauren had read a story about Paul McCartney, who, when he was at the height of his fame with the Beatles, would put on an old jacket and wander into stores like Boots, and Woolworths (which was department store) without donning a single disguise. By not 'being' that person he walked about without recognition for most of the time.

She also remembered the story of how Marilyn Monroe would do the same kind of thing, but when she wanted to be recognised, would 'turn on' the superstar charisma and end up being chased by paparazzi.

The stranger downed his soft drink and left without writing down a single note or taking a picture.

'That,' said Nathan as they tucked into their ice-cream., strawberry for her, vanilla for him, 'was a reporter from the Edinburgh Chronicle,' I've seen him at some of our events.'

'He didn't seem to recognise either of us.'

'No, because in his mind he was looking for a tall, astute businessman, well-groomed and subtle, capable of jumping a fence with a single bound. What he actually got was a slob in a shapeless t-shirt that could have concealed layers of fat, and a long-haired woman whose face he couldn't actually see, who'd had her hair pinned up previously to show off her classic cheekbones. He saw two plebs, that's what he saw.' Lauren looked at him admiringly.

'Nathan King, you're quite a psychologist in your own way.' Once more it hit her, that despite the sexual intimacy of barely an hour before she did not really know this man. Despite his solid frame he was somehow a thing of light, shade, and elusive because of this.

He did not have an alcoholic drink, of course, but he treated Lauren to a gin and tonic. By this time, despite the light outside, time was getting on. He looked at his watch.

'Time to get you home.' By this time, of course, the reporter was gone. They tidied up and got ready for the long drive home. Lauren had to wait while he rearranged the seats using the automatic system and was almost disappointed when she climbed inside and the car was no longer a makeshift bedroom..

The drive back was not filled with a great deal of conversation. When they did talk it was about the work he had done to prepare the show, and how she could assist him with his business. They had a few laughs over the events in the pub, and prior to that as well, but on the whole Lauren did most of the talking.

All too soon, from her point of view, Craigton came into view, and he drove down the long, somewhat basic road that led to her cottage, the place that she now called home. It was good to be back again and she had a sudden surge of relief that she was here, the business needed a lot of hands on work, and even though she trusted her co-workers (she never thought of them as employees) she needed to make sure everything was well. With a start she realised that she hadn't been in contact with them for more than twenty-four hours. No-one had called her, which she took as a good sign.

But inwardly she remonstrated with herself. How could she have been so neglectful with everything that was going on? In truth she had been so absorbed in the man beside her that she had forgotten about much of her life here for a whole day, something she would never have thought could have happened.

She got out of the SUV assisted by her handsome companion. She knew that it was all supposed to be about what was inside a person, but she couldn't help thinking, as she saw his profile, that it was a marvellous thing just to look at this gorgeous man who had made such beautiful love to her. She walked demurely to the door of her cottage, unlocked it and went inside, laying down her other outfit, and turning to speak to Nathan only to find that he was hovering around the front door.

'Come in handsome,' she said, 'I don't bite, unless you want me to,' she added lightly. He grinned at this but gave a little shake of his leonine head.

'Hate to say it Lauren, but I can't hang around, I've had a great time with you, but I have a lot of business to do, a great many calls to make.'

'Stay here and do them, and we'll have another night together.' He wagged a finger at her, but gave smile that showed he was thinking of what had transpired earlier.

'Sorry, no can do, all my stuff is at home. Still, it was fun.' She did something she would never normally have dreamed of doing and pouted a little.

'If your work is that important,' she walked towards him wiggling her hips a little. In her experience men did not easily give up on the temptations of the opposite sex, especially after what the two of them had experienced together. She looked for a range of emotions that should have been struggling across his face, but his handsome features suddenly became impassive. Here was a man, it seemed, who could put his feelings into different compartments. She grabbed either side of his head and kissed him long and hard on the lips, but although he seemed to enjoy the experience, he did not respond as she wanted. He put his hands on her shoulders and gently pushed her away.

'I'm sorry, Lauren, I really have to go, I have a few calls to make before it's too late, and a mountain of paperwork to complete. Whoever spoke about that thing called the paperless office was joking.' She was starting to become angry with him now.

'Go then, go and do your paperwork if it means that much to you.'

'Well it does really, I'm self-employed, if I don't get the correct paperwork done I get in trouble with the tax authorities and I have to file a report with them every month.' Lauren blinked.

'Wait a minute, I run this business, and I only have to hire an accountant every year to make sure my returns are in by the start of April.'

'Yes, but I get paid a lot of money for a big show like the one you've just seen, and believe me, the tax man wants to know the ins and outs of the whole thing.' He held up his big hands, 'do you know what? I'm boring myself even talking about this stuff to you. The crux of the matter is that I'm going to be busy for the next few days. I've had a great time with you Lauren, let's not spoil it now.'

'Well when are you going to bed?' she asked, cursing herself inwardly for being so needy.

'Not until about three in the morning the way things are going, and no, I'm not going to come back here from town and spend the time with you. I still have to be up early. Look, we've got a scheduled meeting on Thursday, I'll see you then and we'll have some fun afterwards.'

'That's right, lover boy, just pick me up and put me down as you like, as if I'm one of your fences,' Lauren tried to speak lightly as if she was making a joke of the whole thing, but in truth she was starting to feel quite offended by his attitude, it really was starting to seem as if she was part of his business, and she didn't like the sensation.

The fresh air of summer, the scent of the apple trees and heather growing outside her cottage were wafting in on the balmy air of the later evening. Often, in such weather, after a hard day's work, she would sit outside and just let the evening scents and sounds waft over her, but now these were a symbol of loneliness, all she would be left with when he was gone.

Suddenly he was holding her in his arms, pulling her close to him. She drank in the smell of his body, a body she had so recently explored with her own. Her breasts were crushed to his chest and for a moment he quite squeezed the breath out of her. She was not a small woman, but his size and strength made her feel as fragile as an egg.

'I really want to be with you,' he whispered in her ear, his voice suddenly low and husky with emotion, 'but I had made many arrangements before – this – happened and I can't just throw them over at a whim.' Then he let her go and was striding decisively back to his vehicle. He nodded to her with only the faintest hint of a smile, got into the front seat and drove off, performing the act so swiftly that he was gone, bare seconds after he had left her side.

Once more Lauren did something that she would have considered impossible just a few days before, she went out to the road that led past her cottage and watched him go, the fingers of her left hand to her lips, her right hand raised to give him one final goodbye.

Chapter Eighteen

Slowly she walked back into the cottage, shut the door, and leaned against it before bursting into tears. She remained like this for a few seconds before standing up straight and squaring her shoulders. This was not her; she was a different person from this, wanting a man so much that she was going to throw aside every rational thought inside her head. Of course he was a wonderful looking man, tall, muscular, and good at love-making. Rational Lauren said 'so what?' breaking through the cloud of desire that filled her mind at the merest thought of him. She had nearly – not quite – begged him to stay with her, and fill her bed for the night. Once more Rational Lauren with a capital 'R' broke in and she decided that she really had to do something about this.

The first thing she did was to lock the front door, go through to her bedroom – how small it looked after their fancy hotel suite – and fling off the fancy new outfit that she had allowed him buy for her after being bamboozled by his fancy language. Naked, she walked into her rather rural bathroom, where even the tub looked too small. She didn't even have a shower, there hadn't been one when she moved in and the cost of having one installed was prohibitively expensive at a time when she had to make extreme savings just to keep the business going. So she put on the hot tap and simply had a stand up wash at the sink. She dried herself off with a fluffy towel that would have done justice to the Grand hotel – she would stint on many things, but never on towels – went back through and dressed in practical clothing right down to her utilitarian white undies. She donned a check shirt and fastened her hair back with a purple band, completing the ensemble with faded blue jeans and work boots. It was just past nine pm by then, but she had messaged ahead when she was on the drive home and the yard, although closed to the public was still manned by one of her co-workers.

Instead of taking the car that she hadn't driven for the last couple of days, she took a stroll down to the yard where she met up with Julie, her chief assistant, who had taken over the reins while Lauren was away.

'Good to see you again,' said Julie. 'It's a bit later than usual, but knowing that you'd be back, I prepared Jewel, she's all ready for you.' She tilted her head to one side and looked at Lauren in a manner that could only be described as perky. Julie was a married woman, just a little older than her boss, but she was all female when it came to knowing about what was going on.

'What?' asked Lauren, seeing the way her assistant was looking at her titular boss woman.

'Well, you had a whole two days and one evening off with a handsome guide, what was it like?' Lauren immediately knew what was being asked of her, but something held her back. Maybe it was the glitter in Julie's eye, or the fact that she didn't like talking about her personal life. This had worked for years because quite frankly there had been very little personal life to discuss.

'I had a wonderful time,' she said.

'Did he wine and dine you?'

'Yes.'

'And then?'

'I think you want to know a few details, if I'm being frank,' said Lauren, 'you want to know if there was something between us?' She took a deep breath and responded to her assistant's expectant look. 'Yes there was. It was, I can't tell you how much, it was wonderful.' She looked at Julie. 'Look Julie, this is neither the time nor the place, I'm tired.'

'I bet you are you naughty girl,' said Julie. 'I saw the pictures you know.'

'What pictures?' demanded Lauren, a sudden chill passing through her body that had nothing to do with the evening air around them.

'It ran in one of the dailies. Caused quite a stir you know. He looked magnificent jumping over that barrier, and it must have taken some strength to restrain that bucking horse. You looked gorgeous in your red outfit. The pair of you saved someone's life. The best part was, this morning a couple of reporters came round. I did what you might expect, I sent them off with a flea in both ears, but I suspect they were looking for information about Nathan rather than you.' Once more Lauren was pleased that she had hired such a sensible, if nosey assistant.

'Thanks for that Julie; you really are a pillar of strength.' Julie looked at her shrewdly. 'All right, but I'm only going by example, and you're the strongest woman I know. I'm letting you off now because I've held the fort, and you need to get out on Jewel, but we're getting together one night, along with Yasmin and a bottle of wine, in your cottage, and we're all going to have a good long girly chat. You have to promise.'

'I promise,' said Lauren so solemnly that Julie laughed.

'He's probably waiting for you at the cottage right now, am I right?'

'I have to go,' said Lauren after a perceptible pause, 'time's getting on, thanks again Julie, and you've done more than you were called for, it won't be forgotten.' Once more Julie tilted her head to one side.

'Lady, we have some serious talking to do. I'll see you soon. By the way, if he's gone off home to his own place just like that he's a bit of a bastard.' She turned and went over to her Mini Clubman and got inside, honking her horn and driving off at a speed that argued she already had a pizza and a bottle of wine waiting for her at home.

Lauren went into the stable and fetched Jewel, who being part thoroughbred, always seemed to be a little perky. She whinnied when she saw her owner and indicated that she was up for a little spot of exercise. Lauren led her out into the yard, talking to her all the time in a calm and soothing manner, nonsense phrases that seemed to have the odd effect of calming Lauren herself. She got on the back of her horse, feeling the power of the beast between her legs. Jewel was finely built compared to some of the more placid horses Lauren kept in the yard, but she was still a huge animal.

Together the pair of them ambled towards the Low Meadow, with Jewel picking up the pace when she realised where they were going. Soon they were trotting over the grassy way, Jewel retreading old paths with confidence. They rode around the huge area a couple of times, and then Lauren urged her steed back to the stables. For a few minutes Jewel actually went at a gallop until she was restrained on the pathway as the stable block and office came into sight, and Lauren felt that familiar sensation of enjoyment and adrenalin as she rode, a sensation that made her know that she was truly alive.

When they got back to the stable Jewel was hardly out of breath. This had been just a mild end of the day for her, although she was perspiring a little. Lauren towelled down her precious animal, giving her some fresh, sweet hay as a reward for the night, and made sure she was comfortable in her stall before locking up and heading back down to her cottage. By that time of night it was starting to get dark although there was still plenty of light to guide her back home.

She had calmed down a lot by then, and although there was an ache in her, a longing that she could not identify, she was tired enough to sleep through the night. She went inside, undressed, donned her practical PJ's, the one with the pink teddy bears on them (she wasn't a girly girl, but she was feminine enough to have the odd indulgence.)

She was still trying to hold off thoughts of Nathan as she got into bed, but suddenly, as she turned to one side, she realised what her longing was for. It wasn't so much the sex, even though that was a side of him she had enjoyed more than she was prepared even to admit to herself. No, it was the fact that even after one night in his arms; she ached to be with Nathan again, to feel him in her own arms, his firm body against hers. As she thought of him in bed with her she let her right hand drift down between her thighs barely touching her most intimate place. She was tender and felt like continuing, but decided not to, knowing that she could well work herself up into a fervour that would over tire her.

Yet at the same time she could picture Nathan back at his apartment in town, sitting there in front of his computer answering in turn a load of emails generated by his work, and the mountains of paperwork that he had to deal with. Because he was one of the organisers, at the very least he would have to write a report on the event and what had happened that day.

Oh, her thoughts were so restless! She was never going to sleep, the memories of him were filling her from head to toe, and she wanted to be with him, his mere physical presence enough to calm her down. How she would love to drift off to sleep in his arms, although judging by their history together, limited though it was, they wouldn't sleep for half the night, as their bodies would be entwined for a great deal of that time.

She was tempted to get up and call him, see how he was getting on. She would never sleep at this rate, the thoughts of him flooding through her. She resisted the temptation to call him; she didn't want to be that kind of woman, seeming to be irrational. She knew from life events that her friends had gone through, that the surest way to lose a man was to seek his attention all the time. What was wrong with her? Perhaps even one text just to say she was looking forward to seeing him again? Once more she had to resist the temptation to grab her mobile phone and do that very thing.

She would never sleep!

Chapter Nineteen

Birdsong came through the barely open window as she opened her eyes and looked blearily at the alarm clock beside her bed. It was about half six in the morning, meaning that she had slept for nearly eight hours! She normally rose early anyway; there was so much to do in the yard even before the arrival of the first visitors that she often got up at six just to get on with her day. She rose, got dressed in her utilitarian clothes that she wore for her job, had a breakfast of rough oats made with semi-skimmed milk and flavoured with a couple of teaspoons of runny honey to give her a morning energy boost along with the slow-burning oatmeal, complemented by a cup of tea flavoured with milk only. Then she went to work.

One of the things she found with being the owner was that she had to work harder than anyone. There was plenty to do just to maintain the horses and she had fine muscles just from mucking out the stables alone. As she got to work on this necessary part of the job she could not help grinning to herself, she wondered how much Nathan would desire this sweaty female in old jeans with her hair tied back, who was quite literally shovelling shit?

Had her weekend trip actually happened? Even though she had returned with him just the previous night, the rescue of the rider, the restraining of his mount, the incredible love-making in the Grand Hotel in Edinburgh, the strange inn, the science-fiction car bedroom: all of these things seemed like some weirdly detailed dream.

Only the pleasurable ache in certain parts of her body, and a lingering memory of his musk, told her this was real. These encounters between them might have ended, but she knew that if she had her way there would be more of the same. They had a business meeting on Thursday, but if she did what she wanted the business they conducted afterwards would be of a more personal nature than the other dealings.

Julie arrived at 7 am, looking a little tired, the result, as she later told her employer, of sitting up late eating crisps along with a rum and coke and watching catch-up soap TV. They greeted each other like sisters who had always got on with each other.

Shortly afterwards Tom and Marianne, the two younger workers arrived. Technically they were late as both were supposed to start at 7.00 too, but they had a great deal of leeway with her given that Marianne had to walk or cycle from a nearby village, and Tom lived on the other side of town, riding in on his new scooter.

As usual at the stables, the day went past quickly and it wasn't long before Yasmin started at nine am. It was Yasmin's task to organise the day, answer the letters and managing the business mailbox. She was really good at this, taking and making phone calls, organising reception and making a whole range of appointments from the bread and butter hacks that kept the money coming in, taking payments and paying bills. If Lauren was the public face of the business, Yasmin was the underlying muscle. The pair of them got on with each other too, which was a huge bonus in such a small business. Lauren was always on call to Yasmin, and failed to answer her bidding at her own peril. This time Lauren gave her secretary half an hour of grace then went in to see her. They greeted each other in a seemingly casual manner but Yasmin gave her boss a significant look as they said their 'hello's'.

'So how was the big weekend?' asked Yasmin raising her well-moulded eyebrows as she spoke, which said volumes more than any words.

'Not you as well,' protested Lauren, already a little weary from being out in the yard, with not enough energy to protest convincingly. 'I'll say to you what I said to Julie, we'll get together for an evening drink and have a girly chat in my cottage.'

'Sounds fine to me,' said Yasmin who was currently unattached, her latest boyfriend having turned out to be a love rat who had absconded with the second woman of choice, knowing that he was going to be ditched when she found out. Lauren had been a shoulder for her to cry on until she had dried up and decided he wasn't worth it. 'So when are you going to see him again?'

'Get back to work woman, we have a lot to deal with,' said Lauren with a touch of humour knowing that she was saying a great deal by not admitting her plans. The fact she could meet up with the girls one night said more than anything.

'You'll be sad to know this,' said Yasmin, sobering up and drawing out a piece of mail that Lauren saw, with a sinking heart, was embossed with the name of Lord Ellerslie's lawyers. She opened the letter and read it with some trepidation. It stated plainly that the good Lord was going to proceed with his action, and he was going to get his lawyers to set the first court date within the next fortnight. The next letter would let her know when she would have to attend the court. He was giving her more time because he was eager to let her settle out of court. Lauren forgot about everything else and gave way to a rather incandescent rage.

'That pure bastard,' she said, 'he really is trying to get his way, what a piece of bad-hearted shit.' Yasmin took the letter off her and gave it a good read. She looked at her boss.

'I guess he's still trying to call your bluff,' she said, 'he keeps giving you more time.'

'I don't care,' said Lauren, 'get on the phone and see if Allan is available.' Allan was Allan Dick, a local lawyer who had dealt with her many times over different matters, such as when they were making a big purchase for the stables, and he was a good, calming influence. Lauren waited in the office while Yasmin made the appointment.

'He can see you at noon at his office.'

'That's ideal,' said Lauren, 'I have an appointment with Peter first. That gives me time for lunch.' She did not have to say with whom.

'You'd better get ready then,' said Yasmin. By then the riders were coming to the yard and getting ready to go out their individual hacks. Because the company did not have a huge staff it meant that appointments had to be carefully managed in blocks of half an hour, so when Lauren left her absence made a major difference to the working day.

'I'll be back from Peter as soon as possible,' said Lauren. She did not have to worry about her staff, even young Tom was well up to the job. She went back to her cottage, dressed in a business-like manner in a navy outfit after having yet another shower – it wouldn't do to turn up at an important meeting all sweaty from her exertions. Just after this she dressed, did her makeup and prepared to go out, and was well on time for her appointment. Lauren was never fashionably late; when she was a solicitor herself she was rigorous in her use of time Then she suddenly had a thought, one that had been on her mind ever since speaking to Yasmin, and took out her mobile phone. She dialled the number under the letter 'N'.

'Hello there,' answered a familiar voice, she was suddenly aware that her breathing was a little short and her heart appeared to be beating three times faster than normal.

'Hi Nathan, its Lauren here. I have some free time at noon if you fancy meeting up for lunch.' There was a perceptible pause at the other line, and his reply, when it came was warm, but cautious.

'Sorry Lauren, I didn't recognise your number. My bad organisation, that is, good to hear from you. Remember, though, I told you I was busy? That's an underestimate; I was up until two in the morning. I really have a great many things to deal with, both in my business and personal life: can we meet up another day? I'm seeing you on Thursday of course to talk about the new layout.'

'I'd rather make it personal.' She said unable to keep the desire out of her voice.

'So would I, believe me,' he said. Her heart skipped a few more beats, for his voice became a low growl now that expressed a rawer emotion. His next words made her heart sink to her knees.

'I have to go now Lauren, I'm just about to go into a meeting with one of the agencies I'm dealing with. Take care, see you soon young lady.' He was a decisive man, no long goodbyes for Nathan, and as the call snapped off she had a sudden temptation to ignore his command and ring him again, interrupting his meeting whatever it was so that he could pay attention to her.

But she was a businesswoman herself and knew that meetings like this could be extremely important, and an interruption might even lose him work. Why, then, was she filled with this impulse to do something so naughty? It was as if something inside her head was shouting 'me, me, look at me, right now!' She was filled with some kind of lingering madness. How dare he go off and do other things on this earth when she was around? Surely she was more important than a few business dealings?

Not-so-deep inside Lauren knew that she had to get a grip; that she was starting to slip into a mode of being that could only be called obsessive. She was not about to make him think she was so obsessed with him. There was no surer way to lose a man than to make him aware that you were totally absorbed in him. She was also aware that if she expressed herself in the way she really felt, he would run for the hills. Then there was the business, he was about to make a deal with her that could be the saving grace for the stables. The hard side of her remained deep inside, and she knew that she didn't want to put him off, but even more than that, she did not want to lose the business.

She put her mobile phone into her bag and went out to her own BMW, which was a much smaller much older one than that owned by Nathan. She skirted the main town and went to Peter Turnbull's offices out towards Galston, a small town on the outskirts of that area. The offices were set in rambling, rural buildings that had originally been a farm, on the road to the town. Peter very rarely kept animals on the premises, but he had his own stable block and a couple of horse boxes he could send out to transport the animals of his clients to people such as Lauren, who could house, look after, and exercise them when there was no space for them elsewhere. She always paid a great deal of attention to Peter because he was a man who had helped her preserve the business, and also because she simply liked him.

He was a big man dressed in the traditional hard-wearing Harris Tweed jacket and trousers, a crumpled blue shirt beneath his jacket indicating that here was a man who never had a desperate need to impress his clients.

'Ah Lauren,' he led her into an office that was more crowded than could have seemed possible, with books and papers everywhere. He was in his sixties and rather overweight but he had a somewhat crumpled charm that immediately put all his clients at ease.

'I've got two fillies,' for you my dear,' he said without any preliminaries, 'I'll arrange to get them over to you at the weekend, at the usual rates, what do you think?' It transpired that the fillies in question were going to be in the forthcoming Ayrshire Gold Cup. It was their first time and for that reason they were not the main focus of the owners, who had others in the race. 'They're still a bit flighty in temperament my sweet, I'm hoping you can work a

164

little bit of your magic and get them in order for me – and the owners.'

'I think I can do that.' Lauren had taken her mind off Nathan long enough to remember what it was like to look after such animals. Even her own staff admitted that she seemed to have a magic touch with nervous horses, calming them down and getting them used to being ridden in a consistent fashion. Turnbull was sending them to her for a specific reason, he knew that she could work her magic, and when they went back to their owners the resulting good behaviour of the animals could only result in a better reputation for his own stock company. He did not have to argue long with Lauren over the details. She liked to bicker with him a little because she enjoyed the back and forth of their meetings, and she always argued about money. He would pay her well in the end, but always looked at the fine detail of what she would provide. He too had a bottom line, she knew, but his business was not always on the edge of crisis like hers. Once the pair of them had settled the negations – the fillies would be delivered early on Saturday morning – he leaned back and looked at her in a questioning manner.

'How are things working out with young Grant?'

'Grant?' she enquired.

'Sorry, I meant our Nathan King,' he gave a low chuckle. 'I feel I can tell you the truth. After the Borders debacle he took it hard, vanished off to his connections in America; changed his name and everything else.'

'So you knew him well before he left, what was he like?'

'Quite a boy, my love, quite a boy. He never stood still, was always looking at the next event and arranging deals all the time. He had to balance this with his desire to impress old Wilson, his daddy. The old man was hard on his choice of career, and the disaster – as Grant or Nathan called it – was an excuse for the old guy to fall on Nathan like the proverbial ton of bricks. I still deal with the old man from time, he owns a few horses, in fact these fillies are his, part of a consortium actually, so you'll actually be supporting the man Grant dislikes more than anyone else in the world.'

'I suppose its business,' said Lauren doubtfully, 'but Nathan is putting work my way, perhaps, ethically I should refuse one or the other?'

'Personally I don't think so. This is purely business and neither needs to know that the other is involved.'

Lauren thought about this for a minute and nodded. As far as she was concerned his words made sense. Anyway this Wilson person didn't own the horses being stabled with her outright, so that was fine. They ended the meeting cordially having made the necessary arrangements both financial and practical. As she was leaving Turnbull forestalled the businesslike handshake and instead kissed the back of her hand then her left cheek. It might have seemed a bit sexist in these modern days, but they had known each other for years and he performed the act in such a courteous old-worldly manner that she could never have been offended.

'Ah you are sweet,' he said, 'a hard business woman mind, and I respect all that, but Grant – I mean Nathan – is a lucky man.'

'What?' Was it so obvious thought Lauren? She thought that she had kept a cool demeanour when talking about her new love.

'I saw the newspaper report, the photographs,' he said, 'it's as if the pair of you, you were made for each other, the way you both looked.'

'Thanks Peter,' she said, hoping that he wouldn't notice the way she was blushing. 'I'll see you soon; I have another appointment, this time with my lawyer.' By this time they were at the front door of his rambling office, he raised a quizzical eyebrow.

'Pray tell young lady.'

'I can't, not until it's settled,' said Lauren. She smiled brightly at her old friend, jumped into the BMW and drove off, not knowing that by sharing she could have cleared up a few mysteries and saved herself a lot of trouble too, but such is the way of life.

She went into town, found a parking spot away from the main street in a residential area. She knew full well that the people who lived in the flats were out working during the day, so she pinched one of their spaces. It was lunchtime by now, but she did not feel eating right now, even though her morning exertions had left hunger gnawing at her. Her mind was on the letter in her bag that weighed so heavily on her mind. She would eat after the business was dealt with.

Instead she walked into the main town, to Bank Street and the offices of Allan Dick, her lawyer. The office was situated upstairs in what had been an actual bank (hence the name of the street) located inside a large building made of red sandstone, along with other similar businesses. On the ground floor was an estate agent, and in the middle a financial consultant. It was quite a climb to his offices up the curving stairway; she had always thought that his clients would have to be fit just to get to him.

She asked the cool receptionist if she could come in a little earlier, and was immediately granted an audience with the great man. Allan was almost the polar opposite of Peter Turnbull. He was a man in his forties with neatly slicked back hair who wore a newish brown suit, and on whose desk the papers used for his business were arranged in neat stacks. She was sure he would know what each and every one of these represented.

'Tea?' he asked, detecting in his almost supernatural way that his client was upset, or maybe it was the fact that she came to see him when she was in trouble.

'Yes, thank you,' said Lauren.

'Please have a seat and we'll have a chat in a few seconds.' He went to the office door and stuck his head round it. 'Saskia, can we have two teas in here please, thanks.' He sat back behind his desk and spread out his hands. 'So how can I help you Lauren? May I just say how wonderful you look, the country life must agree with you?'

'It's this,' she fumbled in her bag for a few seconds and produced the letter from Ellerlie's lawyers. She handed it over and he studied it for a few minutes, reading and analysing each word thoughtfully. She watched him do this, 'what do you think?' she asked, trying not to sound too eager.

'It seems to me that once more our Lord Ellerslie is trying to frighten you into giving him access to the Meadows.'

'I can see that, but they're talking about actual court dates now.'

'I see that too.' At that moment Saskia came in with a tray on which reposed two cups, a teapot and all the accoutrements for making a cup of tea. The lawyer thanked her and she departed with an air of cool superiority that showed who she thought was the most important person in this operation, and it wasn't the man behind the desk. Allan paused and poured her a cup of tea, she took some milk but refused sugar while he took milk along with three spoonfuls of the deadly white stuff. She took a sip of her tea, while willing him all the time to answer her question.

'My advice,' he said, leaning back and tenting his hands together, 'is to settle with Lord Ellerslie. Allow him to build on the land and make you a lot of money.' He gazed at her earnestly, noting the tightening of her lips. 'Before you say anything Lauren, it'll save your business for good. The other way, you'll have to go to court in Glasgow to defend your case; it'll cost you a great deal of time and money.'

'What do you think are the chances of us winning the case?'

'The chances are not only good, we'll win, there's no problem there at all.'

'Then go ahead Allan, please.'

'You might think that lawyers are just out to make money from their clients. I've charged you a retainer, and over the years I've helped you with various contracts, so I have made a reasonable living with you as one of my clients. The problem is; the cost of going to court is extremely high. It's not just a lawyer, you know, I have to have a legal assistant and a clerk, I need to record accurately what is being said. In addition the judge will certainly award you the case, but he won't necessarily award you the costs.'

'What do you mean by that?'

'It isn't as if this is a frivolous case, these land disputes are all too common. The judge might find for you, and the both of you will have to pay your own costs. Ellerslie has deep pockets and you don't. You'll be disproportionately affected by the cost of defending the case and he'll walk away whistling with his hands in his pockets, while you'll be at a major risk of losing your business.'

'How can he afford to do that?' Dick leaned forward and stared into her face. 'I am about to say something that mustn't go beyond these four walls, and if it does I will deny every word.' She felt something inside her shrink when he said these words, knowing she wasn't going to like them. 'I think personally that he's being bankrolled by the housing consortium. Remember, they stand to make millions of pounds if they get hold of your land. That's why he won't be out of pocket.'

'Wait a minute, surely that's illegal?' He spread out his hands and made a fairly hopeless gesture.

'It is, of course, and if it was ever shown to be the case it would bring the court proceedings to a major halt. But what can you do?'

'Then we don't turn up at the court at all, we just let him incur the costs.'

'It doesn't work that way Lauren, you should know that as well as anyone. If you don't turn up in court the judge might accept the legal arguments of Ellerslie's team and award the land use by default.' Lauren was now struggling to keep her temper, and he could sense this.

'Look, I'll charge you as little as I can while still making a small profit. We'll at least win the case, and I believe you have new business coming your way through this Nathan character. I suppose Peter's still sending work your way too?'

'Yes he is.'

'Then hopefully we can get you through this, and out the other side. But don't ignore the whole thing. It would be so much easier if you settled.'

'That,' said Lauren, 'I will never do.'

Chapter Twenty

She went out of the meeting in a foul mood, the euphoria of the weekend having quite worn off. Even in the midst of her anger, though, the thought of Nathan tempered the angst. Soon she would be back with him, and although his presence would butter no parsnips, as her mother used to say, he would provide some kind of healing balm to her emotional wounds. She discovered that she was hungry after all, and went into town to purchase a chicken wrap in M&S, and a can of iced tea. It was a sunny day; she would have them out in the open on one of the benches on the main street thoughtfully provided by the town council.

She made her purchases at the counter, and just happened to be looking out towards the main entrance when she saw through the shop window an unmistakeable figure strolling along the main street. It was Nathan! His presence puzzled her because she had been told that he wouldn't be around, however it was later in the afternoon, so perhaps he had managed to free up some of his time to get away from business.

She had a sudden, mischievous thought that just popped into her head; she would follow him along the street a little, and then suddenly call out his name. Just a bit of harmless fun, she thought, one that would show the lighter side of her personality. She put the comestibles into her bag and followed up on the impulse by slipping out of the store. She had a sudden thought deep inside that some people could construe this as stalking, but after the physical commitment she and Nathan had made, she decided that her sudden appearance could hardly count as being that of some deranged, obsessive woman.

Inside her head, though she had a sudden fantasy. In this she met him, and they decided that they would stroll to the local park, which she knew well because she had often played there as a child on one of her brave expeditions into town to meet school friends. As befitted a rural area, it was a big park with lots of trees that had been donated to the town by a local worthy many years ago, and bushes too. She could just imagine walking with Nathan amongst the trees, finding a secluded spot amongst the bushes, lying down on the cool grass and letting him make love to her right there and then. Her head swirled a little with the thought, and then she gathered herself together. No point getting lost in a dream when the real thing was waiting for her outside.

Although she was physically fit, she was far from being his height, so for a moment she thought had lost him, and then saw his darkly clad, lithe frame, much further up the high street. He was obviously heading for the pedestrian square, where stood a statue of a local luminary, a meeting place for people, with more benches where they could sit in the good weather.

She did not have a clear path to get to him. Since it was a lovely day the public were out in force, and she was actually finding it a struggle to go any faster and avoid colliding with mothers pushing prams, children carrying balloons, not to mention old codgers with walking sticks who seemed intent on tripping her up. It was for this reason that she was still some distance away from Nathan, who was standing beneath the statue, when she saw a sight that, despite the sunny day, chilled her to the bone. As Nathan stood there, a young woman came from the other direction so that he was looking the opposite way and did not see Lauren.

The woman, obviously a few years younger than Nathan, and of Lauren too, curse her, was what could only be described as a raven-haired beauty. She was so tall that she reached beyond his chin, and so slimly built that beside her Lauren felt small and somewhat pudgy, even though she knew inside that really she was neither of those things. The girl looked around as if worried that she would be seen and gave Nathan the briefest of pecks on the lips. The pair of them looked happy to be seeing each other for a few seconds, and then their body language took on a serious air as they looked around for somewhere to go. It was clear that neither of them were entirely comfortable about being seen with each other in public.

At this point Lauren shrank into the doorway of a large store, where she was well in shadow, given that it was such a bright day outside. Unwittingly she had chosen the perfect spot for observing what was happening between the unexpected couple. Across the road from where she was standing there was a place called 'Courtyard Café,' wedged between a phone shop on one side, and a Salvation Army charity shop on the other. Even as she stood there the couple, as she now thought of them, walked along the pedestrian precinct in a somewhat hurried manner, both so tall and dark that they looked rather like a pair of vampires trying hard to get out of the sun.

He opened the door of the café and they both went inside. That might have been the end of that, but as they sat at a table near the entrance the sunshine that kept Lauren in thankful shadow was angled at such a way that it illuminated the two of them well enough for her to see what they were doing. The sun was so bright outside that they were probably unaware that their every action was visible to at least one eager observer.

Lauren chided herself for even being here. It wasn't any of her business whom Nathan chose to meet, or why he had chosen to meet them. All they had done with when in their mutual company was enjoy a weekend of unbridled sex. Why, the pair of them hardly knew each other at all. Why should it bother her if he was meeting with another female, even one as good looking as this? She didn't have a claim on him.

She could see now that they were chatting to each other away from the eyes of the public. Also, in keeping with his nature, Nathan was allowing the girl – she could hardly be called a woman, unlike Lauren – to do most of the talking. His expression, what she could see of it from her observation point, told her all he needed to know. This was not a man who was listening to good news.

The pair of them drank some hot beverage together. Lauren presumed it was coffee, although from her vantage point she was hardly in a position to tell, and as they did so both of them lapsed into what seemed to be a moody silence.

'Time for me to go,' said Lauren out loud so that she startled a passing granny.

'What dear?'

'Nothing,' said Lauren hastily. But despite her own wise words of counsel she was rooted to the spot. Once more she reminded herself that he was not hers, had never indicated that he wanted anything more than to have sex with her, proving that he was a perfectly normal male, and that she should just get on with her day. So why was it that once Granny McNosey moved on, Lauren once more was lifted her eyes to the scene unfolding in front of her?

The coffee finished, the young lady was engaging Nathan in more conversation. This time, from her looks and gestures she seemed to be a little more strident, as if she was urging him towards a course of action. Although he remained largely impassive, the girl made great use of arm and hand gestures, at one point grabbing him by the upper arm while making one of her impassioned pleas. Lauren could not fail to notice that he pulled his arm away from her and felt a strange sense of satisfaction as he did so. Then the girl stood up and faced Nathan. She made a gesture that was so unmistakeable that even Lauren could read her motions from a distance. The girl touched her abdomen, holding it with both hands, and then made a sweeping gesture downwards. Looking at her Nathan said nothing, a grim look on his face telling Lauren that he'd had enough. He threw some money on the table, nodded to the young woman and stood up.

The girl kept talking and grabbed him by the arm again, Nathan still looked grim and shook his head. However he hugged her, speaking to her in what seemed a gentle manner. The pair of them conversed for another minute or so, and then he looked at his watch, gave her a kiss on the cheek, and headed for the door of the building. He turned and spoke to the girl again before leaving, but she barely lifted her head to look at him as she sat back down and stared at the table.

They say an eavesdropper never hears well about themselves, but in this case she was a spy, at this moment Lauren earnestly desired to sink into the ground, especially when Nathan

178

emerged and strode down the main street. He was looking straight across as he opened the door and for a moment she thought he had seen her. Fortunately he was coming out into the sun and therefore she was still concealed by the shadow. He turned and strode down the main street for a few seconds, took a sharp left turn down an alleyway that she knew from experience led to the large, pay car park in the middle of town. It was obvious that he wasn't going to hang around.

For a moment Lauren was gripped by two mad impulses. The first made her want to chase after him, and confront him in the car park, the second made her want to go across to the café and have a word with the young lady. In the event she did neither of these, she decided to return to the stables and do something useful with her day. She went back to the car, and as she was walking up Portland Road, heading towards the residential district where she had parked her own vehicle, a large BMW with tinted windows passed on her right side, which meant that the driver might not have seen her as he paid attention to the busy traffic. For a moment she felt a wave of emotion sweep over her in which anger mixed with love and even a trace of fear.

He wasn't hers; he never had been, despite their wild weekend of lovemaking.

She went back to the car, finding the wrap and the drink as she fumbled in her bag for her car keys looking at them as if they were foreign objects. She had to keep up her strength so she ate the wrap and downed the drink before moving off but the food was like cardboard in her mouth and the drink was bitter sweet.

Twenty-One

One of things she had been able to do in her working life was keep a secret. She declined to have a ladies night that evening with Yasmin and Julie, saying that she was too tired, but promising to get together with them on Friday night. She knew that her meeting with Nathan on Thursday would resolve things one way or another, and either way she would need some form of release. Yasmin was intuitive, immediately sensing that the business was in trouble.

'What happened with Allan?'

'Our lawyer?' Lauren immediately forgot about Nathan in the white hot anger that was building up inside her. 'I'll ask you; what do you think his advice was?' Yasmin studied her employer carefully. She did not even have to guess the result, 'you know, maybe he's right. The business'll be secure, none of us will have to worry about the future if you accept Ellerslie's terms.'

'You too?' Lauren shook her head. 'I've already given you plenty reasons for refusing to sell. Prepare to be a witness Yasmin. I'll be co-opting every one of you in my defence, although to be honest I shouldn't have to be defending my business for nothing.'

'You're right,' said Yasmin. 'Of course there's an easy way out. You could murder the old bastard.' There was a heavy silence, and then the pair of them burst out laughing.

'Hate to say this, but you're right,' said Lauren, 'the way I feel, at this precise moment I could do that very thing.' Yasmin looked at her carefully.

'There's something else you're not telling me.' For a moment Lauren was tempted to burst forth with what she had seen in town. She knew Yasmin would be entirely sympathetic, would even give her good advice, but at that moment she could not bear to share the tidal wave of emotions inside her. The truth was, she felt hurt and betrayed.

'I think the behaviour of our good Lord Ellerslie is enough,' she said. 'Besides I have some good news, Peter's having a couple of new fillies brought over on Saturday morning, I'll be grooming them for the Gold Cup.'

'I know,' said Yasmin, 'he called me about it shortly after you made the agreement. Well, they couldn't have chosen anyone better. You're a natural horse woman; I don't know why you ever left the show riding business.' She realised what she had said, but just looked at Lauren with her big, expressive eyes.

'The horses are fine,' said Lauren, 'it's the people who're the problem. Well we'll start organising things so that we're ready when the court date comes thorough. You'll be able to rearrange all our appointments and bring in some temporary staff while we're away?'

'It'll be expensive to do that too,' said Yasmin, 'but that'll be fine. We can use the money we get as a retainer from Nathan and your profit from the new fillies to pay those expenses. You won't go into the red that way.' Lauren felt her heart sinking again at the thought. Any profit that she might have made was going to melt away just to keep the business going. For a few seconds she experienced such a deep degree of despair that she felt like walking out of the office and working for hours until she exhausted herself just to get rid of her negative angst, or even just walk out altogether and never come back. Instead, mentally and physically she straightened her back and squared her shoulders.

'Yasmin, you're a wonder, I really don't know what I would do without you and your common sense. I'll leave all the bureaucracy to you while I just get on with my own work.' They gave each other a meaningful look. Girls night was going to happen despite being postponed for the moment and Yasmin would be relentless under the influence of wine.

***

That day and the next were relentless. The one way for her not to worry was to get into the business of working directly with horses. She did everything that she asked her staff to do, mucking out the stables, transporting the bales of feed with the tractor from the shed where they were kept, up to the yard, where she would split them up so that they could be fed to the horses in a ritual that was carried out two or three times a day. She also supplemented their feed with oats and other grains mixed with molasses to keep them feisty and put a gloss on their hides.

One of the biggest comforts she got from the whole situation was the horses themselves, and in particular Jewel, her own personal lady, whom Lauren rode first thing in the morning and last thing in the evening before retiring to her cottage. The feeling of this huge, warm, lithe wonderful beast between her legs was like nothing else in life. When she urged her horse to a full gallop down at the Low Meadow the both of them really came alive. Being with Jewel was a way of enriching her life and returning to the fundamentals of what she believed in.

Lauren was not unaware that with her hard work she was subliminating her feelings for what was happening with regards to Nathan. For the first day she had to constantly fight the urge to call him and have it out with him over the phone. She knew that was a bad idea for two reasons. The first was that in a sense what she had seen in town was really none of her business. The second was that being in touch over the phone was in truth no substitute for actually looking someone straight in the eye. Her alternative was to go into town and confront him, once more over something she had seen by chance, but she was seeing him in a couple of days anyway at that point, and once more it really wasn't her business, she kept telling herself.

He could wait.

Also, there was a sort of grim anticipation in her mood. She was going to confront him in a more subtle way, insinuate the topic into the conversation and find out what he had to say. So when Thursday came, the big day, it was almost a surprise to her. She was aware as she ate her breakfast, then went out on Jewel, that her stomach was full of butterflies at the thought of seeing him again. They had barely spoken to each other since the previous week and she chided herself for being so obsessed with this man who obviously wasn't as bothered about her as she was about him.

Not expecting him until lunchtime, she did do one thing that tickled her sense of humour, that morning. Horses are large animals and they eat a lot of hay along with oats and other supplements, in consequence they produce a large amount of dung. This had to be mucked out, of course, but Lauren had a business brain and it had occurred to her that they were missing a trick, She had, a couple of years before, invested in some printed, opaque bags featuring a logo of blooming roses, and now the dung, instead of being put into a heap and wasted, was shovelled straight into these bags. She had negotiated a price with her local garden centre, and the product sold well because it stored easily and was great for the garden.

Dressed in her old clothes, wellies on, rubber gloves up to her elbows, sweat running down her forehead and dripping down, shovelling dung, she had a mental picture of what she would look like to the urbane Nathan, and suddenly found that she was laughing out loud at the ridiculousness of the situation. How could he desire her when she looked like she had been dragged backward through not just one, but many hedges? She was dressed in her mucking out clothes of several years vintage. Young Tom, who was helping her to fill the bags, gave her a sharp glance. His boss often puzzled him.

'What have I done now Lauren?' she insisted on all her workers calling her by her first name.

'It's not you Tom, I was just thinking of how lowly this would look to certain people. I'm seeing an important client in about two hours, imagine if he could see me like this?' Tom did not answer. He was semi-smart in his old jumper and robust jeans, but then he had to take visitors out for a hack in a short while, while Lauren had to carry out a physical transformation.

'I'll let you finish off here,' she said, 'I'll have to get changed, can't let him catch me like this.'

'Catch you like what?' asked a familiar voice, one that she had been longing to hear. They had been to one side of the yard bagging up the horse's product now she looked up and saw that Nathan – curse him – had turned up early. A picture flashed into her mind of what she must look like, her in her scruffy clothes, rubber boots on, still clutching the metal scoop she had been using to fill the bags, stained yellow gloves up to her elbow, while Nathan stood there, impeccable in a morning suit, fresh white shirt, a tie with a silvery sheen that seemed to glint a little in the burgeoning sunlight.

'You're early!' she exclaimed, knowing that her voice was suddenly shrill to her ears.

'Is that the way to greet an esteemed client?' he asked, more than a trace of humour in his tone.

'I'll have to ask you to wait,' said Lauren, 'please finish up here Tom, I have to go. I'll be back in a little while Mr King, in the meantime you can go to the office, Yasmin has just arrived, she'll take you through the details. I won't be long.' She marched in the opposite direction, went round the side of the stable block and jumped into her car. She headed for the cottage, jumped out, had a quick wash, straightened her hair with a furious comb, and applied the minimum of makeup. Barely twenty minutes after she had left her erstwhile business partner, dressed in a fresh blouse, but wearing slacks instead of a skirt, she was ready to see him again on her own terms. It wasn't long before she was back at the office and as she walked in the front door she could hear Yasmin laughing and giggling like a schoolgirl as Nathan chatted to her in low tones she couldn't quite hear.

She could see her own face reflected in the door window and realised that she was starting to feel angry, there was a flush rising to her fair features that some might have called quite becoming, yet she was aware that she was feeling a mixture of anger and jealousy. What did Yasmin think she was up, to flirting with this philandering businessman? Yasmin, she thought, was being totally unprofessional. She found the two of them at Yasmin's desk, a pair of dark heads leaning over some paperwork, still laughing. They both looked up as Lauren entered the main office. It was not a huge space and her riding boots thumped on the hard wooden floor.

'Ah, you're back,' said Nathan with a warm smile. 'Well it's been a pleasure talking to you Yas, hopefully we'll see a lot more of each other.'

'I'm sure we will,' Yasmin batted her eyes at him. Curse her for having such lovely long eyelashes and such beautiful dark skin, thought Lauren, now not entirely in control of her thoughts. He knew the effect he had on women and it looked like he was enjoying using his power to maximum effect..

'I thought we might start by taking a tour of the grounds,' said Lauren, her voice sounding unnaturally high even to her own ears.

'That sounds fine.' She noted that in contrast to the rather nice suit he was wearing, he had on a pair of dark riding boots. He

even managed to make these look like some kind of accessory.
'See you Yas.' He gave Lauren's assistant another smile, and
Yasmin nodded to him with an open grin that showed her lovely
teeth. Lauren decided that she was going to be businesslike as they
walked together out into the sunshine.

'I thought we could ride out together,' he said, seems the
best way to get around your acres of ground.

'Fine, I'll get the hands to saddle up Shadow.' She was
about to call over Fiona, who was already busy, but Nathan shook
his head. 'I think I know how to saddle my own steed Lauren, how
are you anyway?'

'Fine, thanks.' She left him to saddle her own horse, Jewel
was pleased to be ridden again, feisty lady that she was.

It was a most un-Scottish like summer they were having
that year, with long, bright warm days, but she noted a few dark
clouds on the horizon. That wouldn't put her visitors or the horses
off, any rain would be short-lived. It wasn't like the winter months
when the time spent dealing with visitors was much shorter. The
summer was when her business made most of its money.

'I'll show you where you can possibly situate your new
facility,' said Lauren. They rode away from the main buildings and
down towards the fields beyond. Nathan glanced at her from time
to time but she stubbornly refused to meet his gaze as they rode on.

'Look, if it's about this morning, I had time on my hands after getting everything done, so I decided just to come along. I knew you would be working, sorry if I caught you at a bad time.'

'Like you say, as a client you're entitled to come along when you want,' said Lauren stiffly, 'I'm sorry if there was a certain lack of professional polish in my appearance, but you have to understand these are working stables and jobs just have to be done. I was just about to go away and get ready when you arrived.'

'No-one understands better than me,' said Nathan with a little chuckle that set her teeth on edge. 'Jobs with jobs, eh?' he gave another laugh at his own pun that made her want to clonk him one on the back of the head. By this time they were in an area that flattened out towards her precious Meadow.

'I thought this would be an ideal spot for you to set up your experimental arena,' said Lauren. 'Most of our horses aren't up to the level of those used in national eventing, but they're good enough to test your fences, and of course you can build as many test projects as you want.' He looked at the area with a thoughtful eye.

'Yes, I can see that. There will have to be some construction work of course, to begin with, but not a huge amount, mainly putting in the posts for the fencing so that we can screen off the area. I'll be using interlink fencing, but I'll make sure it's green to blend in with the area, and I'll need a site building for office and toilet facilities. I'll need to get the odd delivery lorry down here with materials, but yes, this looks good to go. Thanks Lauren, you'll be well rewarded for this. I know how much it means to your business.'

'I'm glad I've helped you fulfil you're desires one way or the other,' said Lauren. 'Yasmin will help you make any arrangements; we don't need to see each other much if that's what you want. You'll get on well with her, she's a lovely girl, I'm sure she'll see you get everything you need.' She felt the colour rise to her cheeks again as she spoke, what was it about this man that roused such a combination of rage and desire in her?

'She's a nice young lady,' said Nathan, 'but I think I need to deal with you a little more directly. Now that the arrangements are being made I hope we'll be seeing each other a lot more.'

'When do you think the building work can start?' asked Lauren, 'I want it done as soon as possible.'

'I'll get my surveyor out this afternoon,' said Nathan. Was it her imagination, or did his voice sound a little flat, some of the warmth seeping away? Perhaps he was responding to her manner. Quite frankly, she had been cold-shouldering him even as they spent time together. 'I thought we could celebrate by going out for some lunch later.'

'Well that would be good Nathan, sounds excellent, but as you saw when you arrived I was busy, it's a busy time altogether.'

'So where is your cottage in relation to this site?' asked Nathan, 'just so I can ask my site foreman if he needs to see about anything.'

'I'll show you,' said Lauren, 'you see those trees over there, if we ride straight over it takes you to the road that runs past my home.' She raised an expert hand on the reins and with a touch of her heels on Jewel's flanks, rode away from him without another word, aware that she was being a little churlish, cursing inside her mind for what she was doing. Nathan was not in the least phased by what she was saying. Riding after her, Shadow caught up with an easy canter, he was soon back at her side. The pair of them rode over what turned out to be a steeper hill than she had expected so that by concentrating she was less furious by the time they got there. They were looking down the road at the cottage. She was feeling guilty by now at her treatment of this man who was going to help solve her financial issues, and besides, after their longish survey she was thirsty.

'Let's go for a cuppa,' she said, 'as you can see your site foreman won't have too far to go if he needs to contact me personally, if I'm at home, otherwise he'll have to call me, or go to the office.'

'You know as much as I do that mobile phones are not always an ideal solution, that face to face meetings are much better. For instance he might want you to look at a blueprint.' They tied the horse to a nearby wooden fence, and were walking together as she was talking and were approaching the door of the cottage. She put the key in the door, unlocked it and they stood outside for a moment. She was acutely aware of how much he stood over her, making her humble abode seem to shrink behind her.

'It's not much,' she said, 'excuse the mess, I didn't have much time to clear up after having to rush and get ready to see you' There was a faint, unspoken accusation in her voice, it was he that had put her in that condition.

'I hate to say this Lauren, but seeing you like that in that yard, you were, I wouldn't normally use this word with someone with whom I work, sexy.' She turned, startled and looked at him, feeling that he was mocking her with those deep brown eyes. 'I really mean it, your hair was everywhere and you looked grounded, earthy and real. It was at that moment that I really fell for you. I knew you were the woman for me in more ways than one.' Lauren stumbled backwards as he advanced, then felt a sudden surge of anger as she looked at him, standing there so tall, handsome and self-controlled. Something inside her snapped, she turned, ran inside, slammed the door and locked it behind her.

Twenty-Two

'What the hell?' He said from the other side of the door. 'I was only going to hold you in my arms. After what we've been doing, that's not much of a stretch.'

'The hell with you,' said Lauren, a sudden white hot rush of annoyance pushing the words out of her, 'why don't you go and see your girlfriend instead?'

'What the heck are you talking about? I haven't been involved with anyone since I came back to the old country.'

'Really, you're sure of that?' the words were coming out of her in a choking manner now, so hot was her rage she felt as if she would strike him with a dagger if she opened the door, for lying to her in such a blatant manner.

'Open the door,' he demanded.

'You know what, Mister Big Time, I'm thinking of telling you to take your contracts, to go to hell and get out of my life.'

'Lauren, let's talk like adults.'

'Nathan, push off, I'm angry with you after what I saw, go to hell!' There was a pause, and she was expecting him to start berating her, but when he spoke again it was in a low voice with a growl of anger in it. Now it seemed as if, when she opened the door he would want to tear her head off her shoulders.

'I've had enough of this. I thought you were sane, now I know how crazy a bitch you are, I'm glad I found out before things went any further. It's been good knowing you Lauren, have a nice life.' It was so quiet out here, in the countryside that she could actually hear the sound of his big body turning, the scrunching of his footsteps as he stepped on the rather rough path by her home that she glorified with the word 'road.' Soon he would mount his steed and gallop off. Her back was to the door as she heard this, and her heart was pounding so hard she thought it was going to burst from her chest, make a spectacular leap across the room. In a blinding flash she saw that she was not just sacrificing the man, she was scuppering any chance she would have of saving her stables in the face of Ellerslie's legal action.

She was going to lose everything. Worse still, all this was going to go. She would be able to keep her cottage, maybe, but she would lose the horses, the stables, even her wonderful staff who had worked so hard to keep everything going. Despite her personal feelings she knew what she had to do. She unlocked the door and found herself running after the powerful man who was striding rapidly away from both her and her humble abode.

'Nathan, wait, please stop,' for a moment it was as if he hadn't heard her, or as was more likely, was ignoring her plea. 'I'm sorry, it was just that what you did angered me so much I just couldn't hold it in.' Unwittingly this was the one thing she could have said that would make him halt, which he did, turning to scrutinise her with features that were not just displeased, they were dark with anger. It looked as if he really did want to rip her limb from limb, and she felt a shudder of real fear. Then his face took on a more neutral expression.

'I ask you again, what the hell are you talking about?'

'Not out here, come inside,' she turned and strode back to the cottage, knowing that this was a make or break moment, that if he followed her she was at least going to save the stables despite any personal feelings she might have towards what he really was as a man, a duplicitous, two-timing bastard. She should have known better when she got involved with him, powerful men were all the same they just took what they wanted and went on with their lives leaving a trail of destruction behind them.

She was so sensitive to sound that she heard his heavy, angry breathing as he strode behind her, and she was barely inside the cottage before he was in there with her. If she thought he looked big outside, once he was inside the front room of her cottage he was huge, looming, she suddenly felt almost elfin beside him. He was not a man who blustered. He stood there with a scowl on his face as he waited for her to speak. He did not try to sit down on her somewhat worn couch and neither did she invite him to do so.

'Look, personal feelings aside Nathan. I want your business, which, along with other deals that are coming to me will save the stables, so I apologise for my burst of anger. It's the first time that's ever happened. You can communicate with me in future through phone calls and texts and we'll be professional about this. You don't need to see me again in person. Yasmin will have any personal meetings with you, I'm sure she'd love that, given the effect you have on women.'

'I don't know what's wrong,' he said, his face hardening as he searched hers with his penetrating gaze, 'but there's something going on, can you tell me what it is please?'

'Look, I'll sign any papers you want and we'll get this done, then we'll get on with our lives. Thanks for helping keep the business afloat.' She was going to end her words there, hoping to keep him as a customer, but a question was suddenly wrenched from the depths of her soul and the words popped out of her mouth before she could help herself: 'who is she Nathan? Who is she? How many months gone is she? When is she having your baby?'

'What the - ?' this time he couldn't even string together a coherent question, his mouth hung open comically like a fish waiting for a hook. Then his mouth closed, but only for a second, and he did something that to her was quite extraordinary, he burst out laughing. It was possibly the worst thing he could have done at that moment, Lauren's fair features turned livid, with anger, not with embarrassment this time. She tried to brush past him, heading for her bedroom where she would lock herself in. His reactions were lightning fast; he grabbed her by the arm and pulled her to one side so that she sprawled on her own couch in a most unladylike manner. It was a good thing she was wearing slacks or she would have shown more than her anger. He loomed over her.

This is it, she thought, this is where I'm going to be killed on my own couch by a good-looking homicidal maniac.

'I am going to ask you how the hell you jumped to your conclusion,' he said. 'Answer me truthfully.'

'I saw you,' said Lauren even as she sorted out her body, hands pressing into the couch cushions as she prepared to spring away from him, 'I saw you in town with that girl. There's no denying what you were talking about.'

'First of all, you were spying on me? I have a stalker on my hands?'

'If you must know, I was out seeing Peter that morning, and then I had to visit Allan Dick, my lawyer. I happened to see you up town when I was going for a snack, I saw you meeting with the girl. She's gorgeous, she should be a model, and then I saw you go into the café together, and witnessed your little pantomime.'

'So you spied on us?' his anger was starting to manifest again in the hardness of his features, the earlier humour diminishing.

'It wasn't like that. I was in a shop doorway, the longer I stayed there the worse the situation became I just couldn't step out; you would have seen me and thought I was doing the thing of which you're accusing me. Besides, I saw it all Nathan, when is she due?'

'It is actually none of your business,' said Nathan.

'I think it might be some of my business,' said Lauren, 'you took me away for the weekend, you showed off your fancy display, you took me to a grand hotel, you seduced me, we made love. I thought there was something more to us, and then I find out about – this.' She burst into tears, sobbing into her hands.

'You really cared? You wanted more from us?' his voice was suddenly softer, gentler than before. She looked up, her eyes still dim with tears.

'What do you think?'

'Lauren, you should just have asked me.'

'You mean the girl isn't pregnant?'

'Oh she's pregnant all right,' he said. Lauren started to rise and he pushed her back down by the shoulders. 'Listen to me will you? Her name is Zena, she's my sister.' That was when it all fell into place, a puzzle solved in one blinding flash. She could see it all now, the height, the looks, the same dark eyes and the body language. These were people who seemed close because they *were* close, with only the closeness that can be found in siblings. Now

Lauren sat where she was and felt a wave of despair sweep over her. She looked hopelessly at the ground. Then she lifted her chin in sudden defiance.

'I'll take your word for it Nathan.' She stood up again and faced him. 'Do you know what? I've made a monumental fool of myself, I am so embarrassed, but if you're lying to me I swear I'll make sure you won't be able to walk properly for a week.'

'No, honestly, she's my wee sister,' he said. 'She's a great girl, it's a long story involving a holiday romance and a two-timing good-looking rat who met her whole she was out in Greece modelling for a catalogue,' He looked at her with eyes that were suddenly dark, unfathomable. 'You were concerned about that because you thought I had another woman? I've told you this before Lauren, since coming back here I've been too busy to bother with another romance, until last weekend.' He shook his head as if he too was really seeing the light. 'And you swear blind that you weren't stalking me?'

'Do you think I have time to chase men around when I have a business to run?' How could she tell him the truth that she had fought the urge to see him again from the moment he left? That if she had left the impulse unchecked she would have called him twenty, thirty times instead of just once? That she had been dreaming of him constantly and not in a good way for the last two days until her resentment, rage and jealousy had built to a point where she had to let it erupt? No, it was better to let her question stand. He looked at her carefully.

Twenty-Three

'I guess not, I'll believe you, thousands wouldn't,' his tone was suddenly lighter. Lauren stood up and faced him, her face still flushed.

'I –I don't know what to say to you. I've made a fool of myself, you would be justified in taking the business away after what I've done, and I wouldn't blame you. You must think I'm an idiot.'

There was a space between them now because he had stepped back to let her stand up from the couch, but instead of agreeing with her and turning to go away he stepped closer. In the heavy silence between them after her words she was sure he could hear her heart thundering.

'It's not like that at all. Why do you think I manoeuvred to come and see your cottage? I'm an experienced man, I would have known where to send the foreman; the lie of the land didn't confuse me at all.'

'Why would you do something like that?' he did not answer but came even closer so that her breasts were touching his broad body. She did not say anything because it was as of the pair of them became electrified into action. He shrugged off his silvery grey jacket, and threw it down on the armchair in the corner. She grabbed his tie and pulled his face down to hers so that they could kiss, which they did long enough for a minute to tick swiftly by. He pulled back, and unknotted his tie using both hands in a one swift motion, then pulling off his shirt. She had already taken off her own jacket and blouse by then (she was used to changing quickly as the events of the morning had already proven,) and stood before him in her bra. He uncovered her large breasts with one sweep of both hands and cupped them in his large palms. He was a designer used to handling large objects, and he manipulated her breasts with expert ease, bending his head and sucking each nipple in turn as she threw back her head to soak in the thrill of what he was doing.

Bringing her head forward again, she could see that he was excited by looking at the distended nature of his trousers, but just as she was going to push against his large bare, chest with both hands, to leave room for her to kneel in front of him, he bent down on both knees. She had a large, blue woolly rug in front of her old-fashioned fireplace and it was this he was kneeling on, so his knees would be preserved despite the wooden floor, With one swift motion he yanked down her black slacks, with the added bonus that her underpants – solid pink M&S ones – came down at the same time so that he was face to face with her fair bush. She had always been reluctant to shave that area, feeling that her pubic hair was part of her.

She knew from experience that this adherence to nature would not put him off and with her slacks at her ankles; he remained kneeling before her using his tongue to probe her already wet and willing lower regions. She moaned aloud with sheer pleasure as his darting tongue flicked back and forth across her clitoris.

'Stop, stop,' she moaned. He looked up at her.

'What's the matter, am I doing something wrong my love?'

'No, but I want this to be better.' She pulled back from him and sprawled a little on the couch as she tried to remove her boots. He was a willing participant in this process, looking at her in a lewd manner as he pulled them off and flung them carelessly in a corner.

'Lock the front door,' said Lauren, her breath coming on long gasps. She was known as a liberal boss and it was not uncommon for her workers to knock briefly and walk in when they had some kind of news to impart. It would not do for young Tom to walk in and find his employer stark naked as she now was, and in the throes of sexual intimacy.

Nathan had used the time after locking them in to completely remove his own clothes, and was once more naked in front of her. She was sprawled back on the couch and wide open for him. He was far from reluctant to provide her with the pleasure she sought as he knelt down and impaled her on his large cock. He thrust into her so hard that she thought he couldn't possibly last, but their lovemaking went on for about half an hour longer, not that she was counting, and they did things in her small front room that she would never have envisaged happening there in a thousand years.

At last, when they came to a shuddering halt with another mutual orgasm, they just fitted on the couch together, lying there naked, entwined in each other, reluctant to move in the sleepy aftermath of making love on a summer's day.

'I love you,' she said, regretting the words the moment they emerged from shapely lips. Good way to scare him off, she thought. He pulled his head back and looked long and deeply into her fair features.

'I love you too,' he said sleepily, and then he tucked his head into her breasts and actually fell asleep. She stroked the mass of thick hair on his head and found that her cheeks were wet with tears of joy.

***

Nathan did not sleep for long in his post-coital power nap and when he awoke began making overtures to start the whole business again, but this time it was Lauren who was sensible, the fire between her thighs and the hurt in her head having been assuaged by his vigorous love making.

'Let's go back, they'll be wondering why it's taken me so long to show you a patch of field.'

'All right, and I have a lot of work to do to arrange this business anyway, I have to speak to my contractors and get them up here to do a proper survey.' They both vanished into the bathroom in turn to sort themselves out. With his day suit on, and a quick comb of his luxurious hair, Nathan looked exactly the same as when he appeared at the yard barely two hours before. He was, if anything a little more relaxed. In Lauren's case, things were a lot different. She had to scrub off in the bathroom and her hair was a mess. She retired to her bedroom and sat in front of her dresser mirror preparing herself for the return to the stables and as she brushed her hair and put on her makeup she saw a woman who was invigorated by her recent encounter. She was brighter than before and the bags under her eyes from her sleepless nights were fading, for she too had slept. Even more than that, there was a glow about her that had been conspicuously absent when she got out of bed that morning. She was a woman on fire. She shrugged on her blouse and went back through to where Nathan was standing, waiting for her a little impatiently. Men, who passed a hand through their hair and were ready to go, didn't understand why a woman had to prepare for her public even though they loved the results.

'Let's go,' he said. They stepped outside the cottage and for a moment Lauren felt dizzy as the sights and sounds of the world hit her. Everything seemed so overwhelmingly real; the trees were greener in their summer plumage, the sound of the birds was louder, the deep smells of summer drifting on the warm breeze and even the texture of the path , the loose gravel scrunching beneath her boots as they went to their respective steeds, riding at an unhurried pace to the stables.

'I don't want to say anything about – us – to the others yet,' said Lauren. 'It's not because I'm ashamed, it's just that I have a complicated situation going on at work, legally speaking I mean, and there might be a hint or suggestion on the part of some people that I could use our new relationship to help me. Believe you me, that's not going to happen. Besides I want to know more about the situation between you and Zena.'

'It's not something I've been able to discuss with anyone but her,' he said, 'because it exposes a family situation with which I'm not happy. The world being the way it is nothing is ever perfect, but I wish things had been settled with her. I don't want to intervene, but I might have to.'

'What do you mean?'

'Well the truth is that when I went off to do my own thing, when I was barely twenty, my father disinherited me, thinking that by doing so he would bring me back into the fold, so to speak. At that point I was still learning the business and getting to know the right people. I refused to play ball so he told me at our last meeting that I was dead to him, that he didn't have a son.'

'That's horrible. You must have gone through some hard times dealing with the way he treated you.' Nathan stared straight ahead as they rode on. His pace quickened as he forgot for a moment that she had to urge her own steed on to keep up with him, and then he saw her moving forwards and slowed down as he relived the painful memories.

'You have to understand, my father is a tyrant who tried to make us totally reliant on him. I hate to say this, I'm a lot like him, I have grit and determination, I like to make things happen, and he's a highly successful man who always seems to get what he wants. Zena is fine woman, I'm very proud of her, but she doesn't have a career as such. It seems a cruel thing to say, but our father is elderly, and she stands to inherit much of his fortune, she doesn't want to be cut out of his will, especially when she has a child to take care of. It's a dilemma I don't need in my life.'

'Where is she now?'

'She's living with a female friend in town, not far from where I met her.'

'Then I'll make you an offer Nathan, let me deal with Zena, and talk about what we can do. She sounds as if she needs a woman's touch, and she's not the first young woman I've helped out with this, one of my stable lasses found she was in a similar situation a few years ago. I smoothed things over with the family, and she has a bonny, bouncing boy. She brings him up to see us from time to time and he loves horses.'

'Yes, well she wouldn't listen to what I had to say,' said Nathan gloomily, 'in that she could make the entire issue go away. I was happy to fund any medical procedure she might need.'

'Nathan!' Lauren was shocked to her roots, given that she had an ethical resistance to such things, but his face cleared as he looked at her.

'Don't make a moral judgement about this, I respect new life as much as anyone, but if it had been her choice I would have respected her wishes, I was just there to help her out at a time of need. In fact I'm quite looking forward to being an uncle given I don't have any of my own.' Lauren was tempted to say that this could change, but wisely held her tongue. Given the previous misunderstanding between them she didn't want to say anything that might frighten off her new man.

'Set up a meeting between us and I'll see what we can do.'

'All right, but I'm busy getting all the work done on my new project, I don't know if I can stay for long.'

Twenty-Four

The very next day he came and fetched Lauren in his shiny black
BMW, taking her into town to an area near the centre, parking
close to the bank, and leading her to a slightly dirty white doorway
placed between a wine shop and an estate agent. He rang the
buzzer, explained who was there through the intercom, and the
door was immediately buzzed open, then the two of them went
inside. The stony corridor inside led to various flats, and he
knocked on the first door. Zena opened up promptly and invited
them both inside without any hesitation. Nathan made the
introductions and the two women sized up each other. It was one
of those instinctual things; the pair of them immediately
recognised kindred spirits in each other. Inwardly Lauren laughed
at her idiocy for thinking Zena might have been Nathan's
girlfriend. She was almost as tall as her brother and her face,
although thinner was unmistakeably cast in the same mould.

'How's it going sis?'

'Not bad, just making arrangements for a new gig while I
still can, my agent has a local shoot – in Glasgow.'

'Good, well paid?'

'Not in the big league, but good enough. Because I'm not a
fashion model, I get mostly work for the kind of catalogues you get
for free in your Saturday newspaper.'

'I'll help you out,' he said, 'if you need anything.'

'I'll let you know.' She turned and smiled at Lauren, 'do you want a cuppa?'

'Of course,' said Lauren.'

'Not me,' said Nathan hastily, 'I have some field work to do.' He smiled at them both and Lauren felt her heart swelling as she gazed at him. He looked so solid and just – big – in this small place, filling the whole flat with his personality. 'Have fun you two, I'll pick you up later Lauren,' he nodded to them both and departed. Lauren was rather stung that he did not kiss her goodbye, but she figured that he was feeling awkward in front of his younger sibling.

'I'll just make the brew,' said Zena, going into a kitchen about the size of a postage stamp, putting the kettle on. 'Coffee all right for you? It's instant, but a good brand. Have a seat.' It wasn't long before Lauren was sipping her milky coffee and sitting on a long, green couch beside the young woman. She did not have to wait until the chief object of the visit was broached.

'You really adore Nathan, don't you?' asked Zena.

'He's all right,' said Lauren with a mischievous smile.

'Oh he's more than that,' said Zena, 'he's absolutely gorgeous. I adore him too, you know. I'm not obsessed with horses the way he is, but I used to follow him around as a little kid and I can ride fairly well – he made sure of that. He was always so patient and kind to me, encouraging me in every way. Dad was annoyed when I went into acting and modelling, but Nathan helped me with every choice.'

'He's a good guy,' said Lauren.

'If you've got him, keep hold of him,' said Zena, 'you know, you're the only woman I've ever met who he was happy to introduce to me. I always had the feeling that the women he chose were secondary to his career, but you, I don't know what it is, you're different.'

'I don't know about that,' said Lauren, trying to pass off the moment with a light laugh.

'You're so lucky,' said Zena, then her lower lip trembled; she put down her cup with a slight clatter. 'I met what I thought was the love of my life. I was out in Greece,' Lauren kept very still, she knew some of the details from Nathan, but wisely kept her own counsel, knowing when to remain silent. 'Mikos, he was our tour guide on the mainland, he was boyish and so charming.' Lauren knew this was a crucial moment in her relationship with the young woman. She also knew that Nathan would not have engineered this meeting unless he had some kind of faith in her, so she did the thing she was best at and said nothing. It was obvious that Zena was gathering up her nerve, and even though Lauren knew the subject, Zena was not aware of this.

'The truth is, even though I'm not a top-class magazine model, I'm tall and good-looking and I've been told that men are intimidated by me. I haven't had many boyfriends since sixth-form college, and certainly no-one like him. He went after me as if I was the only woman on earth, and when he managed to get me alone I let him…' her voice trailed off. 'Normally I would have waited, but we had such a short time there that it just seemed so natural. Everything else was part of the experience, the sun, the good food, the laughs and he was so charming. I suppose you're judging me.'

'No, not at all,' said Lauren, 'why would I? We've all thrown caution to the winds at some point,' she had a sudden flashback to the events in her cottage a little over a day ago.

'When I got back from the shoot I quickly realised I was missing my period. It wasn't something I'd thought about much, you see, I just knew that I should have taken some precautions but I didn't. There's literally no use going over the same thing again and again, but I did. First I tried the number Mikos had given me. It worked when I was in Greece, it was the way we arranged out meetings, and then it didn't work. It must be part of what he does you see, changing numbers once he's done what he likes.'

'What a bastard,' said Lauren. She saw a flash of temper on Zena's face that emphasised her resemblance to her brother. Then Zena calmed down.

'Sorry, I felt a tide of resentment there when you called him that, you see I think part of me still loves him.' This was her cue to dissolve into tears. Lauren had never been pregnant, but from experience with friends she knew it was a time when a woman would be in the grip of certain hormones that could make her moods volatile. Lauren put down her cup and in the most natural way in the world, put her arms around Zena and held the younger woman until the tears stopped. Zena eventually sat back, wiping away her tears with a tissue from a handy box on the table.

'So you're going to keep the baby?' asked Lauren.

'Yes, it's my body, it's not the baby's fault that its father is missing,' said Zena almost fiercely. 'The only trouble is, the modelling work will dry up, and I'll be too busy afterwards with my baby to work, at least for the first six months, and modelling never paid enough anyway, not for a long term future.' She twisted the tissue in her hands. 'I need to tell my father and look for his support, but I'm not sure how he'll take it.'

'He sounds like a bit of a tyrant,' said Lauren.

'He's not really, but you see he's a land owner, he always let me go off and do what I wanted, but this news, I really don't know how he'll take it, I think he always thought I would be married and settled in a few years. He's quite old-fashioned. I don't know how he'll take it if I'm a single mother. It could go either way. The trouble is, I stand to inherit everything and if he cuts me off I'll be bereft. I can't live on my savings.'

'So you haven't told him yet?'

'No, because I'm afraid.' It was at this point that Lauren drew in a deep breath and squared her shoulders.

'Would it help if you had someone to support you, to put your case as it were?' Zena, who was dabbing at her face with another tissue she had taken from the box, stopped and stared at Lauren.

'You would do that for me? Why? What's in it for you?'

'To be blunt, I saw you with your brother. He's a decent, upright man and he means a great deal to me. Also I saw his interaction with you, and from what I've seen he would do anything for you.'

'But the one thing he would like to do, he can't,' said Zena, 'because he's cut off, out of the will. He doesn't care, of course, he's made his own way, but he doesn't want me to end the same way. I'm not like him, I always loved the estate, I grew up there and I love the countryside, I don't want to lose that. It's not about money, it really isn't.'

'Well I'll tell you what, I'll come with you, and we'll discuss the matter with your dad. What's his name?'

'Ewan, Ewan Wilson, Wilson is our family name.'

'Fine, well I'll go with you and we'll discuss the events with your father. I'm sure he'll be supportive of you.'

'That's the problem, things could go either way. He'll chide me for being so stupid, as he sees it, and he'll complain it will ruin me for marriage.'

'Look at you; you're gorgeous, young lady. Child or not, you'll get a husband, and why would you even want one anyway? Honestly, men!' This was the right approach because Zena burst out laughing through her tears and the pair of them bonded even more. About half an hour later Nathan came back to the flat to fetch his passenger, and he exchanged a few fond remarks with his not-so-little sister, before taking his lover back to Craigton.

'Thanks for that,' he said almost absently as he drove towards the stables. 'Means a lot to me.' She knew right away that this was high praise from him because he was a man of few words.

Twenty-Five

He proudly showed her the nascent construction site. There was a neat portakabin to one side and a pile of fencing that to her untrained eye seemed far too much for what he wanted to achieve. Large vehicles were at work, both bringing materials to the site and taking away the soil. A small digger was at work scooping out the holes for the wooden fence posts. There was a huge cement mixer that was in constant use, with men feeding in with spades the sand, cement and gravel that was used to make the material that would hold the posts in place. Lauren realised what kind of person she was as she watched the men at work. She had a sudden longing to be in there wearing her jeans and an old t-shirt getting on with the work.

'You don't mess around,' she said, looking at her large companion with nothing but admiration on her pretty features.'

'There's no point messing around,' he said stolidly, but there was a look in his eyes that said he was pleased with the progress his men were making, 'This is small potatoes compared with getting the jumps ready for a large show, they should be finished within the next couple of days, because basically all we're doing is making a bounded outdoor arena.'

'Well you've done a sterling job Nathan, why don't you come back to my cottage and we can talk things over.'

'I think I would like that.'

***

They were hardly inside the door before he slid his arms around her, but she slipped out of his grasp, turned and locked the door from the inside, then turned back to the man who had become her lover. He held her in his arms. She had almost forgotten how firm his grasp was as he pulled her to him and enveloped her more than she would have thought possible. In his grasp she felt safe and warm, yet at the time there was a hardness to him that had nothing to do with his physical state (that hardness she could feel pressing into her, exciting her.) She felt that his mood could alter at the turn of a coin, and she responded to his demanding mouth that seemed almost to be seeking to devour her. She was not going let him go, that she felt, but at the same time she knew this was a man who would follow his own path, no matter what.

After a while, although he did not seem to grow exactly tired of their passionate kiss, he more wanted to move on with the business of making love and pulled off her top to expose her breasts still in their bra. He pulled aside the red silken fabric of her bra (she had worn it deliberately thinking that this very thing might happen.) Leaving her bra on her he bent his dark head, sucking on each nipple in turn. She felt her pussy getting wet at the very thought of him and was almost wishing that he would leave aside this part of their lovemaking and get straight down to entering her. With her few other boyfriends she had always needed a great deal of foreplay before she got down to the actual business of having full sex, but there was something about this big man that made her want him inside her as soon as possible.

He got to his knees, lifting her skirt and pulled aside her panties exposing her hairy pussy, again pushing forward with his head so that he could lick her exposed clitoris. The nipples of her exposed breasts were rock hard by now, and she grabbed his thick, dark hair with both hands, holding on to him as wave after wave of sensation went through her body. She was breathing in loud gasps as she kept gripping his hair, but not so hard it would hurt his scalp. Then suddenly she was falling backwards on to her old green couch. He had pulled away from her, stood up, grabbed her by the hips, literally carried her the short distance and threw her down in front of him. The strength of the man to be able to do this! She was not some skinny waif-like model, but a real woman, whom it would take great muscular activity to shift. This evidence of his strength was enough to turn her on even more.

Neither did he hesitate, but unbuckled his wide black leather belt and allowed his trousers to fall to his ankles after having first kicked off his shoes. His Calvin Klein boxer shorts were distended at the front, but he did not seem to have any worries on that issue, because he undid the buttons and his large cock popped out of his underpants, a welcome sight to his lusty lover.

She was still sprawled backwards on the couch, her own flimsy pants to one side exposing her glistening vagina as she put out her arms, inviting him forward. It was an invitation that he did not spur. The couch was low, so he bent down on the rug in front of her and pushed forward with his cock, rubbing it against her entrance, not just to tease her, although it had this effect, but to lubricate the head and shaft of his penis. She gripped his penis, and although her hands were not small it seemed large within her grasp and guided him into her well-lubricated pussy.

She gasped as he entered her, he really was large, but as her vagina accommodated his penis she felt the waves of pleasure return. Strictly speaking the pair of them should have stripped off and gone to her bedroom but in a way fucking like this in the middle of the day was like a stolen pleasure. The urbane businessman and the horse rider were riding together passionately in the dance of love.

His large hands played with her breasts as he thrust into her time and time. He was so big, looming over her it felt as if some primal beast was enjoying the fruits of her body, taking her to heights of pleasure that only a few weeks ago she had never known to exist. She had never known a man who could take her to orgasm before, even in such a short time, and soon she was shaking uncontrollably as she came to her climax. Nathan, who was still thrusting into her at the time soon caught up with her and she could feel his seed spurting into her willing vagina. She put her arms around him and drew him down to her, the scent of their comingled bodies an added pleasure to her, and although he was wearing some kind of deodorant, that musky scent she thought of as man-juice still came off him, which along with the scent of his deep, also somewhat musky after-shave, still sent her senses reeling.

They remained that way for quite a while, it seemed he was not the kind of man who would simply cut and run once he'd had his way. They cleaned up and got ready to leave. She took some obscure pleasure as he opened the door in the presence of this big, indomitable man who was putty in her hands when it came to making love. He turned to her just after opening the door and there was a look on his face that she could not read, as if he was struggling with an inner force.

'The hell with it,' he returned and grabbed her, holding her close, enveloping her in his arms, their bodies so close she could feel their mutual heartbeat.

'Lauren, I've never felt this way about anyone. I'm crazy about you. I've got a hell of a lot to do with the site and setting up this new course, but I'll see you tomorrow after you have a bit of time with Zena. Can I spend the night with you?'

'I don't know sir,' said Lauren stepping back from Nathan and smiling up at him, 'I mean, your big black car in front of my humble abode? It would look like what it was. I mean a girl has to think of her reputation. I'm not sure if I can go that far.'

'Oh come on, I've got a bike I could hide at the back,' he said, 'I could ride up the hill from town.'

'I'm not so sure, you might be tired after all your hard work,' she said, flinging the words across her shoulder as she stepped pertly in front of him.

'Like that is it, you've had your way and now you reject me? How dare you!' he lifted one of his big hands and smacked her buttocks. The palm was so big, and he hit her cheeks in the middle so that he stung both of bottom cheeks at once. Lauren felt a sting from the slap shortly followed by a glow that was not just on her cheeks. She felt a familiar tingling in her pussy and suddenly had a desire for him to grab her, put her across his knee and spank her with the same force he had just used. Her face flushed and her breathing became heavier.

'Let's go back inside,' she said a little hoarsely, but he only laughed.

'I promise, we'll continue where we left off soon enough my love,' contented enough, the pair of them made their way back to their respective places of work.

Twenty-Six

'Things must have been pretty bad between Nathan and your dad for things to come to this pass,' said Lauren as she and Zena made their way out of the flat in which the young woman was staying.

'They were. You see dad had the idea that Nathan would take over the estate when he got to a certain age, say thirty, leaving dad to travel the world. Managing an estate is not as easy as people think; in fact a great many mundane duties take up a lot of time such as dealing with correspondence, managing the land, the attached farms, the upkeep of the many outbuildings not to mention the maintenance of the big house. There's a lot to it. Dad had this idea in his head that Nathan would do the management while he and mum went travelling around the world. They were both in their sixties when this was mooted. Then before they could go on their travels, and when Nathan was doing his own thing, mum had an accident that killed her. She was barely sixty. Dad never forgave Nathan.'

'Why?'

'In a sense he blamed Nathan for mum's death. She was a very practical woman, and she was visiting one of the farms attached to the estate, and driving a tractor that overturned. She died in hospital; Nathan was too late getting there because he was on the other side of the country. Father blamed Nathan, pointing out that if he had taken over the estate – or running it rather – mother would have been on a cruise and the accident would never have happened.'

'I hate to point this out,' said Lauren as they got into the car, 'but accidents can happen anywhere, and your mother chose to drive the tractor that killed her, I'm sorry to say. How could Nathan have protected her in any way?'

'That's exactly what Nathan said. But father would have nothing of it; he was so furious that he cut Nathan out of the will. Yes, just go through town, you're heading for Craigton Hill.' Lauren was too busy thinking of her own father to question these instructions. Dick Holloway had died doing what he liked and Lauren had never once blamed him for doing so. In fact she had taken over the business because of her love for both her mother and father. But no-one would have censured her if she had simply sold up and moved on. She suspected that Zena's father was one of those people who needed to exert control over everyone.

The foreboding of what was to happen did not occur to her until they passed the entrance to her own riding stables.

'Not far to go now,' said Zena in a completely guileless manner that showed she could not possibly sense the turmoil that was beginning to grow in her fair companion. 'Here we are,' she said as they came to a set of impressive gates, painted in black but with the top curlicues outlined in gold. The gates were wide open and led to a long, gravelled drive. With hushed breath Lauren turned into this, feeling and hearing the scrunch of the car tyres on the fine gravel. A peacock strutted proudly near the car, and as she drove on the huge baronial mansion appeared in front of them.

'This is it,' said Zena happily, obviously relishing the appearance of the family home. She turned joyously to Lauren, 'thank you so much for doing this, I can't thank you enough my love.'

***

In some ways the meeting went well, but in others it seemed as if she was walking in a daze, within a nightmare not of her own creating.

'What's wrong?' asked Zena, seeing Lauren's crestfallen expression as the pair of them got out of the car.

'I'm nervous,' said Lauren, 'I never thought I would end up in a confrontation with Lord Ellerslie. I had no idea he was your father – nor Nathan's. I never thought Lord Ellerslie was Ewan Wilson.'

'He is,' said Zena, 'let me explain something about names Lauren. When you inherit a title you call yourself Lord or Lady So-and-so after the title. Dad was born humble Ewan Wilson in Kirkton a long time ago. He was fifth in line for the title of Lord Ellerslie, but one by one the other potential heirs died off and when the old Lord Ellerslie died, dad inherited the entire estate.' By this time they were traipsing across the gravel towards the set of six steps that led up to the main door. 'So Nathan is potentially the next Lord Ellerslie?' Zena looked extremely serious.

'Do me a favour, don't mention Grant, which of course is Nathan's real name. There's nothing more liable to make my father boil over in fury.' By this time they had climbed the main steps and were at the impressive double front door. It had an old-fashioned bell pull and a large iron knocker, painted black like the large door knob. Zena knocked firmly. She did not have to wait long because the left side of the door was opened by the impressive manservant Chivers, whom Lauren had met on her previous visit, The pair of them were obviously expected, because he merely nodded, invited them in and closed the door behind them with a bang that sounded like the thump of doom to Lauren.

The manservant glided forward (it was the only way to describe his smooth movements) stood at the door of the front room and announced the visitors, who went inside, and then he discreetly vanished. Lord Ellerslie, the former Ewan Wilson, stood there looking even bigger than before. Now that she knew, Lauren could see the unmistakeable resemblance to Nathan, they were both big, commanding men, and undeniably attractive.

'Daddy!' exclaimed Zena, running forward with her arms out, her natural joy overcoming her nervousness. Her father's features softened and he embraced his youngest child with real affection. Zena was not a small woman, but she looked like a little girl beside her large father. His expression became enigmatic as he let her go and looked at Lauren with obvious curiosity.

'Well, well, Miss Holloway. You're the last person I was expecting to see.'

'I'm here to support Zena,' said Lauren, 'we're friends, you see, she loves horse riding. We got to know each other through mutual friends.' Zena shot her a warning look but Lauren was not about to fumble and drop the ball now that she was here.

'Why, we can have a chat about various things,' said Ellerslie with seeming joviality. He rang the bell, 'this calls for a drink.'

'Just tea or coffee,' said Zena hastily.

'Same here,' said Lauren, 'I'm driving.' After a soothing cuppa the two women sat across from Ellerslie, who being a far from stupid man sensed that something was in the air. He sat with his leonine head tilted a little to one side and looked at them expectantly.

'Daddy, you've always been good to me, you love me, I know it, but I've got something to tell you, something that isn't easy for me. I am so afraid you'll be angry with me.' A tear trickled down her face.

'My wee lamb, you know how I feel about you, I can't be angry with you.'

'Then I'm just going to come out with it, I'm pregnant.'

'How did that happen? I mean, I know how it happened of course, the biology is pretty basic. What the hell led to this?' It was Lauren's turn to intervene.

'Lord Ellerslie, Ewan, if I can call you that, your daughter has been waiting a while to tell you this. She's a beautiful young lady, and possibly younger in her head than her rather impressive looks would suggest. She was on a shoot for her modelling company, and a young man seduced her. It was a combination of the sun, the sand, the location and his charm. There's no point getting into the where, and why. Other women, some much older than Zena, have had their heads turned by a charming man.' For a moment an image of Nathan flashed in front of her eyes, but she dismissed this and concentrated on her speech. 'Ewan, the truth is, your daughter is frightened of her future and she needs you more than ever, both financially and emotionally.'

'Daddy, I'm scared of your anger at this,' said Zena, lowering her head, the tears flooding forth. Ellerslie sat there looking rather stunned for a few seconds.

'Are you going to see the young man again?' he asked.

'No,' said Zena, pursing her lips together.

'Then I will say this to you. You're my heir and I don't want to lose you. If you keep the child that'll be fine, I'll make sure he – or she – is looked after.' He spoke quietly, even gently, and as if looking inwards, 'after all, you're the only one who'll give me a grandchild. Now, Zena, come here and hug your daddy.' She crossed to him almost eagerly, and he embraced her again. 'Now do me a favour my young lady, please take a walk in the grounds, I need to have a chat with my neighbour if that would be all right with you. We have some business to discuss.' Zena looked faintly astonished at this, but did as she was asked, stepping out of the French window and treading the path beyond that bordered the well-manicured lawns. Ellerlsie turned to Lauren.

'I'll say one thing for you; you're a brave woman Lauren Holloway, given the situation between us.' Lauren felt like a fly trapped in amber, how could she possibly admit that she would have reconsidered if she had known to whom Zena was related?

'Now I'm here, and you've sent off Zena – congratulations on taking things so calmly – I'm guessing you want to talk to me about the property deal?'

'Do you know what Lauren, I want to talk to you about Zena's future? More tea? No? That's fine, I can tell you want to get down to business. You see all this property takes a lot of money in upkeep. I'm at an age where I'm slowing down, and I have to hire people to do everything. The income from my farms barely covers my existing outgoings. This place costs a fortune to heat. You can see where I'm going with this.'

'Yes, you want me to make a deal with you regarding the housing project.'

'It's not for me, Lauren, it's for Zena's benefit. She's everything to me now her mother's gone. We can avoid this court case, all the unpleasantness of that business. All you need to do is let me use our mutual land.' For a second or two Lauren wanted to burst forth with an indignant repudiation of his statement, but she decided to take the high ground. 'Will you consider taking my offer? We'll both be rich, and that you'll be able to live a better life than ever. Why you could even hire someone to run your business, freeing you up to do what you want.'

'Can I have time to give you an answer? Give me a day or two.'

'Of course, but I expect you to drop the court case at least. It's already cost me some money, but I'm quite willing to forgo that for the financial gain that will preserve everything for us both.'

'That's fine,' Lauren called back Zena, who was still walking around and looking at the rather spectacular view of Craigton Hill. Because the baronial mansion was high up, in a setting that took in all the farms around, the riding stables further down, and even the layout of the town. Lauren could understand why she wouldn't want to lose all this, especially with an unborn child. 'Are you staying behind?' asked Lauren, 'I'm sure you'll have a lot to discuss with your father.'

'I'll speak to him soon,' said Zena with a sweet, genuine smile that nearly broke Lauren's heart, 'but I'll have to go back and make sure my friend knows what's happening. She comes back from her job tomorrow and I want to see her in person with the good news. She'll bring me back when we leave.'

'Don't you have your own car?'

'I do, it's being fixed, something wrong with the steering. I get it at the end of the week.'

'Well Zena, I'm a busy woman, do you want me to leave you here with your dad, or will I take you back into town, final offer?' Lauren was struggling with a lot of mixed emotions, but she didn't want to abandon a young woman with whom she had made a strong connection.

'If you don't mind I'll take a run into town, father has a shaky grasp of driving these days. He's all right in the country but he gets a bit close to parked cars in town for my liking.'

'That's fine, I'll get you down then.' The pair of them went into the building and said their goodbyes. Zena was in an up mood, bubbling over with enthusiasm now that she knew her father didn't mind the prospect of becoming a granddad. She was so enthused that she did not notice how subdued her companion had become, probably mistaking her mood for eagerness to get back to work. Zena chatted enthusiastically on the way along the drive. Halfway down they were met with the sight of a man in a green Barbour jacket who was carrying a half-cocked shotgun draped across his arm. The man had rumpled grey hair and waved to Zena who waved enthusiastically back.

'Who's that?' asked Lauren without a great deal of interest, as they rolled out on to the main road. This was the Scottish countryside; it was not unusual to see an armed man going around.

'That's Mathers,' said Zena. 'You must have seen him before, his cottage is close to your stables.' In fact Lauren felt that she had never seen the man before, but then again, both her estate and Ellerslie's were large, and a gamekeeper could certainly live nearby, if he never intruded on her land she would possibly have never seen him. Zena was bubbly and chatty all the way back to the flat. Lauren could not help responding to the younger woman, the pair of them smiling and chatting to each other quite naturally. They parted at her front door and embraced each other, still smiling they parted.

As the door closed Lauren let her face fall and went back to her car, driving off, her expression now far from joyous as she headed towards her riding stables. This wasn't going to be easy, but it was going to be done.

Twenty-Seven

Nathan King was at home in front of the machine that was making him money. It was a top-quality, brand new laptop with a spreadsheet open in front of him. His work involved a great deal of pricing and contracting. This part of the job – sitting in his home office looking at a screen, was not his preferred mode of operation purely because he did not like sitting on his backside for long. Much more to his liking was the formation of the building operation; it was why he had spent so long at the site operation at Craigton Riding School making sure that the work was going well. At this rate the operation would be set up in a few days and he would be able to start building test jumps.

There was also the satisfaction in him that he was able to put some money back into the community. He was paying Lauren well for the use of her land. This wasn't some affectation on his part, he knew that she would provide the horses for the jumps, and would be able to bring forward some good amateur riders who, starting young, would keep the sport alive for the future. Who knew? He realised that she had an indoor centre, but perhaps in due course he could persuade her to build a much larger arena that would attract more business to help to enhance their life together.

Together?

He realised that he was picturing not just a business, but a personal union. For the first time in his life this brought a smile to his face instead of a frown.

It was not a feeling that was to last for long.

There was a thunderous knock at the front door that suggested a muscular man of some twenty stone was trying to batter down that particular barrier. Nathan rose from his office chair, which was a miracle of modern engineering in itself, and went to answer the door. He did not encourage visitors, most of his business was conducted over the phone, emails or personal meetings for a very good reason, this was his private space and no-one was encouraged to be here.

He opened the door and was almost relieved to find Lauren standing there instead of the giant muscleman he had pictured in his mind. He was about to speak when she stepped forward. He had heard of eyes blazing, it was not something he had seen in real life, but it was true. Her furious gaze held his as she stepped forward and slammed the door behind her.

'Careful there,' said Nathan mildly, 'you'll have that thing off its hinges.'

'You bastard,' said Lauren somewhat thoughtfully, swinging her right hand unexpectedly and slapping him on the face. It was a good slap too, catching him unawares and rocking him back on his heels. He was rocked back on his heels in more ways than one, but reacted with the lightning reflexes of a man who had been dealing with horses all his life, grabbing both of her wrists with his large, capable hands before she could do any more damage.

'What the hell are you doing?' he demanded.

'Let go of me you bastard!' shouted Lauren, causing him to kick the door shut with his foot to try and prevent the neighbours from hearing anything. The last thing he wanted was for the police to arrive.

'I'll let go of you if you stop hitting me,' said Nathan reasonably. 'Or should I fling you outside and call the police?'

'You would like that,' she fired at him, her mood blazing up once again, 'get rid of me like you do with all the women in your life, you cold-hearted using bastard. I'd call you a pig but you're not even at that level!'

'I've had enough of this,' still holding both her wrists her whirled her around and threw her down on the red leather couch, which was wide as well as deep and she sprawled back, incensed that she was finding it hard to get up. 'Sit still!' he roared, 'get a grip on yourself woman and tell me what the heck this is about.' Lauren was breathing deeply and her face had a flush that was attractive even though it was caused by sheer anger.

'You know exactly what I'm here for.'

'I really don't.' He fingered his jaw, 'there's going to be a bruise you know.'

'How long did you expect to get away with it?' she asked hoarsely, 'did your father put you up to it? Get a little hold on me so that you could manipulate me into selling the rest of my land? Lord Ellerslie's little lackey, that's what you are.'

'Lauren, look at me,' he commanded, and it was clear that he was holding in his own anger. 'I will swear to you that I have not spoken to my father for more than three years – and I've been in America for most of that time.'

'Why should I believe you?' spat Lauren.

'You can ask the people who commissioned me in the States,' said Nathan calmly. 'I wanted to cut all ties with the old bastard because I knew what a manipulative, horrible old sod he was and is.' He strode over to his phone that sat on the desk, picked it up and threw it on her lap. 'Go on, call anyone you want, I have international minutes, ask them what I've been doing.' The blonde woman looked at his phone, opened the screen and scrolled through some of his numbers, particularly the international ones. For a moment she seemed about to make a call, then put the phone down.

'That housing deal, too much of a coincidence,' she said forcefully, starting to rise to her feet. Damn this couch, it was so big (she suspected it was where he slept) that along with her anger she failed in her intent.

'What housing deal?' asked Nathan looking bemused, which meant he was an extremely good actor, or was genuinely bewildered by her angry reaction?

'The deal he's trying to force me into to allow the construction of more than five hundred new houses between my land and his. It'll make me a lot of money but it'll ruin my business.'

'And mine,' said Nathan.

'What?'

'Well, look at where it would be. I assume you mean the Low Meadow? My riding ground is halfway between there and your stables, I can't create commercially sensitive projects when some arse with a pair of binoculars can spy on me from their bedroom window. It doesn't make sense. Besides the construction work would disrupt my own operations.' Lauren suddenly looked very thoughtful indeed.

'You have nothing to do with this?'

'I honestly didn't know what you were talking about.'

'Why didn't you tell me you were Lord Ellerslie's son?'

'Honestly it never occurred to me. I haven't spoken to the old man for years, why do you think I changed my name?' Lauren put her head in her hands and said nothing but began to sob, not noisily, but to herself, her shoulders slumped as she did so. 'Lauren.' She raised her head, her face wet with tears.

'Once more it all falls on me. I've made a horrible mistake.' She finally managed to get to her feet. She looked at Nathan, who was wearing a rigid expression. His eyes met hers briefly then slid away from her, it was as if he was looking at white space, unfocussed but staring. Her shoulders were slumped, and Lauren started making her way to the door. 'I suppose that's our business ended. If you're telling the truth I've made the most colossal idiot of myself.' Broken, she began to open the door. 'It's court in a couple of days Nathan, I can't guarantee to you that your outdoor centre will be left intact. If your dad gets his way I'll be forced to grant the land for building. Between two hundred and fifty and three hundred houses on the meadows I've loved and cherished since I was a little girl.'

'What are you talking about?' his voice was low and grating, when he turned to her there was an air of real menace about him, and for a brief second she was genuinely frightened. But from his next words it was obvious that the anger was aimed elsewhere. 'You mean the old swine is taking you to court over that land to force you to sell?'

'Yes,' her hand was poised over the doorknob now, and she was half-turned, regarding him with uncertainty. 'The worst of it is, he knows he's going to lose the case, but it will cost me a great deal of money, I'll have to pay all my own court costs as he tries to prove some legitimacy over his claim going back in history. Any money I'm making off you and the new horses from Peter will be swallowed up by the entire business. If they find in his favour I'll have to sell.'

'Why didn't you tell me?'

'At first it was because I didn't want to scare you off as a possible investor, then it was because I wanted you around, and I didn't want to burden you with my problems. I didn't know he was your father, you see, or I would have said something much sooner.' Nathan stepped towards her, and although his expression was still serious, he was not as menacing.

'Come over here and sit with me, we need to talk.' She followed his lead and they sat down on the commodious oxblood leather couch.

'It's no use Nathan, I've ruined everything.' He bowed his head and seemed to think very deeply; when he raised it again he looked straight into her face.

'You weren't entirely wrong about the situation with my father,' her face stiffened in anger and she began to rise, 'wait, sit down, I don't mean I was deceiving you about my relationship with him. The old bastard hates me for being what he is, an independent shaker and maker. He wanted to preserve me in aspic, keep me where I was. He would have loved it after my personal disaster when my name was muddier than mud, if I had crawled back to him to take up the favoured son position.'

'But you didn't.'

'No, I buggered off to America, where thanks to friendships and contacts I was able to make a good name as a course designer. Then I came back here, returned to Ayrshire and started building up my business in your riding stables. It doesn't make sense; most of my business is in the horsey parts of the country, like Midlothian or Dumfries and Galloway. Why would I set up here, knowing he would get wind of it? The only reason I can think of is personal. I wanted to wave my success in his face, goad the old idiot and show him that despite everything he's tried to do, I'm a roaring success. I'm sorry Lauren, I have exploited you, but not for the reasons you think.'

'That's strange,' said Lauren, 'the court case only came about after I started seeing you. But how would he have known about us? What was the connection?' She thought deeply for a few seconds. 'Wait a minute, he uses Peter Turnbull and Peter brought your business to me.' She searched his face for a few seconds, but it was obvious to them both that her sudden insight bore the unmistakeable stamp of truth.

'I'm going kill the old arsehole,' said Nathan, unconsciously bunching his fists, 'I'm going to pound his face to a pulp. Can't you see what I was doing? By setting up here and letting the word get back to him I was saying 'look at me, it's your boy Grant, look what I've become, look at me, I'm dancing. Well, I'll deal with him, and then I'm going to kill Peter Turnbull.' He rose to his feet, breathing heavily. He began to make his way to the door, but Lauren struggled to her feet and went after him. She grabbed hold of his arm, feeling the muscles flex beneath his clothing. He brushed her off like a fly.

'This isn't the way,' she said, 'Peter didn't know! He was just boasting about you, he loves you Nathan, don't you understand? He's loved you since you were little. As for Ellerslie, is he worth it? Don't you like the project – and me?' He paused, turned and looked at her.

'I'm confused about you. You're the best woman I've even known, but you storm in here, haul off and smack me about. You're a firebrand Lauren Holloway. I don't know what to do with you.' The day was hot and there was faint smell of sweat in the air from their earlier exertions, that musky scent again and there must have been some primordial response in her because she was wet again, and her nipples were erect. He too was showing obvious signs of lust, judging by the sizeable growth in his trousers.

'Lauren, you still don't know how much you mean to me?' he stepped forward, grabbed her and held her in his powerful grip. If he wanted revenge he could break her neck with one swift movement, and for a moment she felt a surge of fear, knowing that she hadn't been exactly nice to him at the beginning of their encounter. She was wearing a flowery scent, and he seemed to breathe this in deeply before bending his head and kissing her deeply. She was abruptly filled with a desire that seemed to flood her from head to foot.

'Take your clothes off,' she ordered, pulling back from him.

'What the hell?'

'Strip,' she ordered, already removing her own garments. She had dressed very smartly for her meeting with Lord Ellerslie in a black pencil skirt, black jacket and cream blouse with a white bra beneath. She had also worn tan stockings, not tights, because of the summer weather, so it didn't take her long to strip. Nathan was not slow either, infected by her enthusiasm for was to happen, he too threw off his garments and was soon naked in front of her. She drank in his big body, his muscular arms, his flat stomach, his muscular thighs and the sight of his large cock. Naked, her breasts moving in a manner that could only be described as pendulous, she knelt before him and sucked his cock. He threw his head as she worked his member in and out of her mouth numerous times, holding the shaft with dexterous fingers. At last he could take it no more, pulled back, picked her up with his strong hands and threw her down on the oxblood leather couch.

He moved forward and positioned his large body between her legs with a dexterity that belied his large frame. He did not need to lick her pussy because as her legs opened she was soaking wet with desire. She hardly needed to do so, but moved her right hand downwards and parted the lips of her pussy for him, wide open with desire. With one swift move he thrust his throbbing member inside her. She was not disappointed with what followed as he held her large breasts, licking and sucking her nipples as he thrust in and out of her with a vigour and force that seemed even greater than before. His musky scent intermingled with her own, and for this time of lust they seemed to be truly one. As he thrust into her she held his firm buttocks with both hands, pulling him into her so that she could feel the maximum force of his powerful body.

Then he pulled out of her and indicated that he wanted her to turn around. Still filled with lust she obeyed her lover and turned around, pushing her buttocks out towards him as he impaled her again with his cock. She had not thought that her pleasure could be any greater, but pushed his manhood into her, the different position in which she found herself caused a difference in friction that drove her wild with pleasure. They were still on the leather couch, kneeling on the big cushions and she had to brace her hands on the arm rest at her side as he thrust into her time and time again. He seemed too, to have turned into a primal beast, making grunting noises that expressed his need for her body.

'Oh, oh, oh,' he grunted, thrusting with a vigour she had never known in a man.

'Yes,' she screamed, 'fuck me, fuck me hard you big bastard.'

'I'll teach you to hit me, you horny bitch,' he said, 'take this,' he thrust into her with even more vigour until suddenly he came with a loud groan, his seed spurting into her willing body. She could actually feel him coming, pumping his essence into her, and this spurred her on to her own orgasm, her body quivering with a force that threatened to unseat her from the couch. She pushed backwards to keep his cock inside her as long as possible while her rich, deep orgasm lasted.

His erection began to fade and she gave a small cry of loss as he pulled out of her. He embraced her, muzzling her neck with his hot lips as he pulled away, his hands still grasping her big breasts, fingering her still erect nipples. Then the two of them collapsed, drained by their vigorous love making. They were both covered in a warm sheen of perspiration, and there was a rich smell in the hot air that was not quite one or the other body scent but a mixture of both. They lay like that for a while, and then she ran to the bathroom and had a quick wash. When she emerged he did the same. They both dressed quickly, looking much the same as before. Neither of them said much until finally, looking much the same as they had, they were standing looking at each other.

'What the hell happened?' asked Nathan, 'I'm feeling a bit dazed – and drained.' He stared at her and she could not help giving a mild chuckle.

'Do you still want to kill your dad? Because if you do, you'll have to get in line for me, so I can get in the first blow,' they both laughed aloud at this. Their fury seemed to have dissipated along with their lovemaking, although there was a tacit understanding that they would have to do something about the old trickster. 'Look at this place,' she said. The flat was as small as her cottage, and piles of papers lay everywhere. There was a desk in one corner crammed with notes and paperwork. Boxes of files lay about too and clothes were hung up on one of those free standing racks that contained his suits, shirts and ties. Lauren picked up a photograph album that lay to one side of the couch. 'What's this?' She noted that Nathan bridled a little when she picked it up.

'It's nothing,' he said, 'just a few pictures of my various shows, doesn't mean a thing.'

'Aww,' said Lauren, 'it's showing a sentimental side of you.' She leafed through the pictures and saw a much younger Nathan standing in front of his various constructions, with many different horses, on or beside them. He was a serious looking young man and she could see that he had dedicated his life to the business up until now. One picture of Nathan beside an older man made her stop short. 'What's this, why are you with a gamekeeper?'

'Gamekeeper?' Nathan loomed over her, taking the album from her hands. He looked pained, 'That is the traitor, the man I suspect of ruining my career, Lane Marsh.' He stared at the picture for a second, closed the album and sighed, 'never mind, I've moved on with my life. I tried to find the bugger for ages, but he totally vanished, and I was too busy moving on to my new life in the USA to bother with him anymore.'

'You're wrong,' said Lauren, 'he's about all right. I've seen him today, only that's not his name, he's called Mathers.'

'Where did you see him?'

'When I was with Zena. He's your father's gamekeeper.'

Twenty-Eight

It wasn't long before they were back at the riding stables. By this time it was late afternoon, and it was a good guess that so-called Mathers would be back in his own home having his 'tea' as working class people called their dinner in this part of Scotland. Lauren and Nathan did not say much to each other as they went and prepared their respective horses. The pair of them came out of the stables leading their prospective mounts. The riders were both dressed in jodhpurs and wearing hard hats. There was a rich summer scent in the air carried along by a lingering breeze. It was a smell compounded of the horses, people and the greenery that surrounded them. Breathing in that deep air Lauren had a sudden feeling of contentment as she mounted her steed, Jewel. This was her place, it was where she belonged. Nathan pressed his foot in the stirrup and jumped on the back of his own horse, Shadow, the pair of them looking male and massive in the afternoon sunlight. No wonder Nathan had to relinquish the role of jockey as he grew older and bigger. The size of man and horse together did something to Lauren, tying a strange knot of excitement in her belly.

As if by some psychic bond, the pair of them rode down towards the Low Meadow, the only sound was the deep breathing of the horses and the thud of their hoofs on the deep, soft grass that led to their destination. On the way there they passed the construction site, and the men who were hard at work finishing off the boundary of the practice area. Some of the men stopped and waved at the passing riders and the pair of them waved back. They were soon at the meadow, but instead of dismounting rode around the huge grassy area for a while, giving Jewel and Shadow their heads. Both horses revelled in this sudden freedom and managed to work up quite a sweat even though neither worked at their full capacity. Even the horses had their own distinct smell, a deep musky odour that in a way reminded Lauren of her lover Nathan. This, then, was her as she really was, horse and lover making her complete.

A stark contrast to the real business of the day.

Finally the pair of them slowed down Jewel and Shadow, dismounting once they had come to a complete stop, and leading them over to the tree line, where they were secured by their reins to the low-hanging branch of a beech tree. Nathan thumped the side of his equine companion.

'Good boy,' upon which phrase Shadow gave a deep grunt, nodding his head a couple of times as if in complete agreement. In contrast, Lauren put her arms around Jewel's neck, the pair of them nuzzling together in what Nathan and even Shadow would regard as a sickening display of affection. Promising to be back soon, they moved off between the trees and soon came to a path that led through the very woodland that Lord Ellerslie wanted to remove to build the new housing estate. As she walked, the peace of the woodland descending upon her, Lauren could see why denuding this area would be a criminal act. Some of these oak and beech trees had been here for hundreds of years. Even the Scots pines were fairly old, being in their 80's or 90's. Few people knew this, but some trees actually have a limited life, grow quickly and fall, but those trees can still be about one hundred years old.

Nathan, who hadn't spent much time on his father's estate since he was a teenager, didn't know which direction they had to go, but with Lauren's guidance they soon found the black-tiled roofed, whitewashed cottage in which the gamekeeper lived by tradition. She had seen the cottage before when she was a teenager living with her mother and father. Nathan strode forward so quickly that she almost lost him, but Lauren darted forward too, making sure she was in front of him, knocked on the door and quickly called out to the occupant.

'Mr Mathers, are you in? It's Lauren Holloway.' She could see by the look on Nathan's face that she had stolen his thunder, but she was interrupting for a reason, knowing that she was in the middle of a potentially explosive situation. For a second nothing happened, then the door opened a shade and 'Mathers' appeared. He looked at his new visitor through the narrow crack and his expression was far from welcoming. In the meantime, Nathan, catching on to what was happening, stepped to one side so that he was not seen. 'I've got important information for you about the estate, can I come in?'

'Can't we speak here?'

'No, I don't want to tell you out here,' she smiled at him, and she was a good looking blonde with a dazzling smile, the older man smiled back.

'Come in then miss.' He turned and Lauren followed him inside, along with Nathan who could move with surprising stealth for a man of his size. The door, much like Lauren's, led straight into the front room. There, in one corner of the room near the old-fashioned fireplace stood his shotgun and a box of shells. So-called Mathers turned to invite her to sit down, only to find he was confronted by the two strangers. He took one look at Nathan and dived for the shotgun, only to be tripped by Lauren so that he went sprawling on his own floor. Nathan dived forward and picked up the shotgun. He held it as the gamekeeper got to his feet. As the son of a Lord, Nathan was an expert at using this kind of weapon. He loaded two shells, cocked the shotgun and pointed it at his ex-partner with an ease that argued he knew what he was doing. The gamekeeper normally had a tan at this time of year, now turned as white as milk and held up both hands.

'Don't kill me,' he whined. 'Please Grant.'

'I'm not going to kill you,' said Nathan, 'I just want answers. Lane, how the hell could you do it? I thought we were friends, partners.' He suddenly 'broke' the shotgun which meant opening the body of the weapon, and let the cartridges clatter to the floor. 'Ach, to hell with it. I can't undo the past… come on Lauren, let's go. I'll take this so you don't shoot me in the back. Don't worry; it'll be left where you can find it.' The pair of them turned to go, but they were stopped by a sudden shout from the man behind them.

'Stop!' they turned and found that they were looking at an ashen-faced man who was the very picture of abject despair. 'Load that shotgun,' he said, 'shoot me in the heart, and do me a favour, don't miss.'

***

Barely an hour later a couple of people who were both grimly silent, were riding their respective horses back to the stables. Nathan was like a rock on his mount, big, still, somewhat immobile, with a frozen expression. Only the merest movement of his feet in the stirrups or a bracing of the reins showed that he was still paying any attention to where he was.

'Are you all right?' asked Lauren, and Nathan responded by suddenly kicking his heels into his horses flanks, leaning forward and urging his steed into a sudden gallop. Lauren, who was not slow off the mark, pushed forward, and with a word in her horse's ear, pushed Jewel into the same action. Jewel wasn't as powerful as Shadow, who was bigger and more muscular, but she had plenty of heart, being smaller and lighter, and soon the lovers were galloping side by side on their steeds, Nathan's thick black hair ruffling in the breeze a look of devilish joy on his face, strong jaw outthrust. Lauren's blonde hair was streaming out behind her, the deep scent of the green landscape filling her nostrils and even a faint odour of Nathan as she rode beside him.

Soon they were at the stables, the horses coming to a clattering halt on the cobbles of the main yard. Julie and Tom were there, startled as the two riders came into view. Nathan dismounted, as did his lover.

'I'm glad you're ready,' said Lauren, 'do me a favour Julie, Tom, I hate pulling rank on you, and Jewel is going to fall out with me, but could you take off their saddles, dry them down and get them back to their boxes – ch and reward them with some sweet feed once they're settled down.' She stroked Jewels head for a moment. 'Good girl,' she said, and kissed her on the nose. Jewel gave a toss of her head and whinnied. Lauren looked back regretfully at the horses as she strode away with Nathan. As they entered the big black BMW, her mind went back to their confrontation with Ellerslie's gamekeeper.

***

So-called Mathers stood there for a moment then looked at the pair of them.

'All right,' he said, 'if you ain't going to kill me, Craig, let me make you a cuppa, just had ma dinner' Nathan, however, did not let go of the shotgun, not trusting this former colleague, even when a somewhat battered mug of tea was thrust into his free hand. 'Black, no sugar, just the way you always liked it.' It was surreal to be in this situation. Lauren availed herself of his invitation and sat on a couch that had seen much better days. Now that the atmosphere had calmed down Nathan finally relinquished control of the shotgun, but remained standing and kept it behind him, propped up beside the fireplace. Mathers/Marsh went straight into his story.

'I was a horseman from an early age. Used to get the animals ready for the point-to-point races up here on Craigtoun Hill. My dad was a tenant farmer for the old Lord Ellerslie. That one was a fine gent, a real gung-ho character. He used to come to the farm and poached me as a groom for his stables. Anyway I went back to farming after ma dad died, as we were tenants it made sense, and forgot all about the horses. I kind of heard about the situation with Ewan Wilson. He was already in his middle years when he became Lord Ellerslie, but I knew him from earlier because he often came up to see his old uncle.'

'So you were a farmer who loved horses and he knew it?' asked Lauren.

'Got it in one,' said Mathers. 'Then his boy started becoming obsessed with the animals, and next thing I knew the old guy had recruited me to be a mentor to the boy. He offered me the deeds of the farm if I played a little part, and to tell the truth it was kind of fun. I really enjoyed the travelling bit, and I genuinely loved helping the boy – you Nathan – to set up in your new career.'

'Then why the hell did you try and ruin me?' demanded Nathan.

'I didn't want to sabotage you old son, I really didn't, but your dad came to me one day, just before your big show. He said that if I didn't make sure you had at least a lone major disaster, he would take back the farm and sack me. He said he would ruin me. So I made sure that your big set piece would fail. I made it unstable by removing a few bolts so it would fall over like bit of cardboard.'

'Idiot,' Nathan's eyes were blazing, and for a moment it looked as if he was going to pick up the shotgun again.

'Believe you me, I felt horrible, but my old mum was not in the best of health, and my sister, who was older than me, had to run the farm and look after her. It broke my heart. Then it broke again when Buck was killed and his rider injured. I hadn't meant all that to happen, was just protecting my own interests, but you know what they say about the road to hell.' He stared straight ahead with unseeing eyes.

'I really ought to kill you right now,' said Nathan, 'you could have ended my life chances there and then.'

'But he didn't did he?' interrupted Lauren in the calmest of calm voices. 'You were too strong for that, you picked yourself up and got on with your life away from your father, who had tried to possess you through this man. You don't need to bother with revenge, not on Mathers, he was just a tool.'

'So I was 'disappeared',' said Mathers. 'I went back to my old name and my old life. And it did me no good, no good at all.' He put his hand over his face and gave a heavy sigh. 'You vanished to America with new name, and a purpose, less than two months later my dear old mum died, the cost of the burial was more than my savings. Then guess what? My older sister upped sticks and moved out, seems she had been carrying a secret fancy for a widower on a nearby farm for years. I was left in arrears, and I was sick of farming anyway. It was one of the reasons I took on the horse job and worked with you. Your dad offered me the gamekeeper post with a tied cottage an' I been here since.'

'So you nearly ruined me for nothing,' said Nathan, some of the old bitterness arising again.

'What've I got?' said Mathers, 'no wife, no family, no pension, just a cottage that ain't mine and a load of bitter memories, an' every night I curse what I done to you.'

'Look at it this way,' said Lauren, 'there's an old adage about keeping your friends close and your enemies closer. It looks to me as if Mathers here has lost more than he's gained; he's a victim of circumstances as much as any of us.'

'She's right,' said Nathan, suddenly looking very much like his tall, indomitable father. 'You know what? If I took your miserable life I wouldn't be punishing you at all. The best punishment is to leave you alone Marsh, or should I call you Mathers? Either way it doesn't matter.'

'I'm sorry,' said Mathers, 'it was all for nothing.'

'No,' said Nathan, 'it wasn't for nothing, you see in a way you did me a favour. If I'd stayed in this country, one way or another my father would have found a way to interfere with my life. In driving me to America you really helped me become the man I am. I'm only sorry a horse died in the process. Mathers, I forgive you. You've punished yourself more than I could have in my wildest dreams. Come on Lauren, we have a job to do.' That was when the pair of them walked out leaving behind a broken man. Yet, as she glanced back Lauren thought she saw a glimmer of hope in the face of the gamekeeper, brought there by the forgiveness of the man he had wronged.

Twenty-Nine

It was funny, almost surreal, thought Lauren. The day had started with her anger at being deceived – or thinking she was being deceived – about Nathan's relationship to the man who was the bane of her life. Now they were going to the home of that same man, both with more than a few questions to ask,

She knew that it was her turn to speak up. There was a reason for this. They couldn't just walk in and beard the old lion in his den without facing some kind of resistance. These were both Alpha males, a confrontation was exactly what they were going to experience.

'What do we both want?' asked Lauren.

'What do you mean?'

'I don't even know why we're going here, not really.'

'Because we're going to tell him face to face that he's to get out of our lives. He's going to ruin my new gymkhana and your business if he forces that deal through, and he's not going ahead with that court case.'

'All right, I know what you're saying. You can be a controlled man,' said Lauren, 'I'm the one who flies off the handle. Let's just agree not to respond when he goads us, just to put the facts to him, get him to drop the court case, then we both walk away.'

'Agreed,' said Nathan. By this time the BMW was purring up the finely gravelled driveway until they were close to the building that loomed over them like a minor castle. Nathan had grown up with this, she thought, what other people would have called luxury, yet she sensed it had never been his home. Certainly she had never met him, and her family had been there for a couple of years before he left to start his career.

They got out of the car. Lauren found her heart was beating even harder than when they had been having sex. She understood that this was a crucial meeting for her future. Nathan was admirably restrained, merely climbing the steps to the front door in an unhurried, casual manner, pulling the bell handle and waiting for the response as if he was paying a social call to a neighbour. A few seconds after he rang the right side of the door was opened by Chivers, the smooth-faced manservant Lauren had met on previous occasions, who blandly took their names and asked them to wait.

'I'll find out if his Lordship can see you,' he said silkily, vanishing into the vast interior of the hall. They heard subdued voices in the distance, and then the servant reappeared and invited them in, ushering them into the front room. Ewan Wilson, also known as Lord Ellerslie stood near the French windows looking at the vista displayed on this side of the house. He looked at the former Grant Wilson and gave a brief nod, his expression neutral behind his large, white moustache.

'Ah Grant, welcome. This is most unexpected, have a seat, I'll get Chivers to bring in bring us in some tea, or coffee if you prefer.' He spoke as if his son had just gone out for the day and was returning for a quick chat instead of being parted from him for quite a few years.

'My name isn't Grant, or Wilson, its Nathan King,' said Nathan.

'Neither of us wants a cuppa,' said Lauren. Her firm jaw became even firmer as she stared at the belligerent Lord, 'we're here to ask you to cease and desist with your actions. Right now. You drop the court case and you don't pressure me anymore.'

'And somehow you've managed to captivate my son? I'd heard he was back in the country. I suppose you've managed to inveigle him into your camp with that blonde mop and those not inconsiderable bosoms? The answer of course is no. In fact by coming here with your minder, this could be seen as intimidation. Not something you want to be seen doing in the light of facing a jury in just a couple of days. This will of course be reported to the authorities.'

'We know,' said Nathan, bunching his own jaw and unconsciously curling his fists. 'I know what you did with Buck, and my show.'

'No you don't. In fact I don't have a clue what you're talking about so-called Nathan.'

'Really? Well I've been talking to Lane Marsh, as he was called at the time. He told me everything, how you helped to sabotage me. The thing is, he doesn't know it, but he's going to court to talk about you, how your deal is going to remove his home. The only one he's got. We'll talk about your deal with the builders, and how you're getting backhanders off them. That's the reason you're taking this court case, to force Lauren's hand. I've got nothing to lose. Oh, and by the way if you try to use Zena as a bargaining tool, don't worry about her. I'm going to give her a job on my new project. So cut her off if you want, it won't make any difference.' For a moment the two powerful men stood there in similar attitudes, tall, erect, curled fists. It was an almost silent standoff. Lauren could picture the pair of them on a dusty high street in a Western under the blazing sun, pistols at their hips as they squared off.

There was a strange atmosphere in the room, one of suppressed violence, she could almost smell the scent of what was about to happen between them despite the delicate scent of the lilies in a nearby jar, the smell of Nathan's aftershave, her own flowery fragrance and the almost aggressive cleanliness of Lord Ellerslie, palpable as he came closer, yet there was an underlying, almost cloying darkness between the two men that seemed to fill the air,

261

Lauren knew it needed one more word for the two of them to start fighting, and they were big men, and violence between them would be destructive, they could really hurt each other. She was shocked to find that her pussy was getting wet and her breasts were tingling at the thought.

'You bastard,' said Ellerslie, 'you're going to ruin everything. I *need* that housing deal you moron. You don't understand,' he swept a hand around the space in which they stood. 'When I was a child I grew up in a housing 'scheme' as we called it, and it was a scheme all right, a scheme to crowd poor people together and keep them down. I knew I had well-off cousins but no-one ever introduced me to them, my dad was a fitter in a valve factory, an honourable profession as far as I'm concerned, but as the young brother he was last in line. Then they all dropped off their mortal coil one by one, an accident here, stroke there, until suddenly, at the age of forty, a successful textile salesman, I was in front of a lawyer. You were born just three years later, and we had inherited everything. I became Lord Ellerslie. Humble Ewan Wilson from Kirkton the Lord of the Manor. But all of this needs money. When you need money to maintain something you have to make it any way you can.'

'You can do what you want on your land,' said Nathan bluntly, 'leave us alone.' It was at that point that Lauren knew he was truly hers because of the way he spoke about her business. What was his was hers, and vice versa, she just knew.

'Idiot, they won't build unless I get all the land.'

'Then go to court, but I've got a witness now,' said Lauren, 'I'll be able to allege collusion and show that your claims are in bad faith – and I'll put the name of the builders into the mix. They won't touch you with a pointed stick when I'm finished. I'll lose money, but you'll lose everything.'

'You stupid little bitch,' Ellerslie finally lost all self control, he sprang across the room – and it was quite a room, a huge Edwardian sitting area, so he had to move quite a bit before he could get to her, but before he could reach Lauren, with Nathan already poised to take him on, he stopped, his face flushed and gave a loud gurgling noise, then he sank to the ground, still gurgling. Even as his father buckled at the knees, Nathan was on his mobile phone calling the emergency services.

'He's having a stroke,' said Lauren, who had seen this kind of thing before when she was in training to be a lawyer, when elderly clients got worked up. She ran through, got the manservant, and with his help, and Nathan's they got Ellerslie into the recovery position then waited for the ambulance.

Once the emergency services arrived Nathan stood and watched as his father, now with an oxygen mask over his face, was loaded into the back of the vehicle. His expression was hard to read.

'I'm sorry,' said Lauren, laying a hand on his arm, 'this must be hard for you, despite your feelings.'

'Thanks,' said Nathan, encapsulating all he was thinking in one word. The pair of them left once Nathan had given Chivers a few instructions about what to do with the household arrangements. He was such a commanding figure and stepped so easily into his father's shoes that the aide didn't even think of questioning his orders.

Then it was time to go.

Chapter Thirty

Three months later Lauren was locking up the offices for the night. She had already arranged a get together with Yasmin and Julie for the following night, and the three of them were finally going to have that girls night in complete with wine, snacks and endless discussions about the wedding plans.

She heard the sound of a powerful engine and did not even have to look away from her task (she was saying good night to Jewel) to recognise who was arriving. The powerful black BMW halted and Nathan stepped out, a big, powerful handsome man who gave her the same thrill as before when she turned and walked towards him.

'How is my future Lord Ellerslie?' she asked, feeling petite as she stood in front of him in her work clothes.

'A great deal better for seeing you,' he growled, wrapping his big powerful arms around her and drawing her into his strong body. He was not afraid to show his feelings unlike some of the stuffed shirts she had known in the riding world. They did not have to drive far; he took her down the newly refurbished road that led from the stables to his outdoor arena. Now it was up and running, and with a canopy roof that had been added with her permission so work could continue even in a Scottish winter. She admired everything, from his new jumps, to the special surface suitable for the horses, and the surrounding seats. As a simulation it was everything that could model his new show designs in an effective manner.

'We're doing the first big trial tomorrow,' he said, 'I'd be honoured if you would be first to go round with Jewel. I'll be taking Shadow of course, and that'll be the real test given his size – and mine.'

'I like your size,' said Lauren as the pair of them went back into the BMW, flushing faintly at the inadvertent double entendre. Silently he drove to the cottage. By unspoken agreement he followed her inside and they embraced again. She stepped back.

'Will your father make it back home soon?' she asked.

'He's a lot better,' said Nathan, 'with a bit of work he'll be walking again soon. He's a fighter. I still don't know how you managed to turn him.'

'Turn him?'

'Actually, scratch that. You were a rock, showing up to the hospital every day even though you have a full time job, making sure that you spent a lot of time with him,'

'There was a reason for that. I didn't know all the facts, and when you told me about the state of his finances - '

'Yes, well I couldn't really act for him at the time, but Zena got permission to deal with the estate, and we found he was in serious financial difficulties, that was why he was taking the court case, he was desperate you know. It turns out he was, and still is, in danger of losing Craigton Manor. Even his manservant, the faithful Chivers, hadn't been paid for a few months before father had his stroke.' He gave Lauren another hug. 'You worked miracles with him, talking to him, and after just one week, starting his recovery, cajoling, even bullying him a little, into getting out of bed towards rehabilitation.'

'Nathan, my father was a jump jockey. He had numerous accidents and setbacks in his riding career, and do you know what he did? As soon as he could he got back to fitness, doing his exercises, following doctor's orders, and he came back every time. All right, he was killed eventually in an accident, but he was super-fit for a man of his age.'

'Well, the old git protested at first, but you worked with him day after day, taking him through his exercises, helping him get back.' Nathan stopped speaking and looked to one side, Lauren could see his Adams apple moving up and down as he choked on his own emotions. 'You know, thanks to you and the physiotherapists at the hospital, they say he's on the road to recovery. He'll be in for another week or two, and then we'll get him home.'

'The truth is, I felt responsible for his stroke,' said Lauren. 'I took action, it's what I do. Besides, I some ways I got to like to old beggar, like his son, he has some good points.'

'I'm working through his finances,' said Nathan, 'he'll have to sell a couple of farms, but with some help from other sources – Lauren knew Nathan meant his own cash injections – 'we'll get the estate back on its feet and save the manor.'

'It helped when you got him to give you power of attorney,' said Lauren. 'What led to that turn-around?'

'I was visiting him one night,' said Nathan thoughtfully. 'You had been in during the day. His speech is still affected, but he asked me finally, 'what are your intentions towards that girl?''

'Oh yes?' Lauren cocked her head and looked at Nathan brightly.

'Well I told him, and shortly afterwards he signed the paper to make me his attorney, and he even put me back in the will on condition that I took up the title. You see, I have guaranteed he'll live in his beloved manor for the rest of his life.'

'So what was it you told him that made him change his mind about you?'

'Lauren, it's hard for me to say this. My career is my life. The new ménage, the trial runs, the construction, I'm going to be away for days, even a couple of weeks at a time, I need a woman who can cope with that. What I told my father was simple enough.' Lauren held her breath. 'I told him I intended to ask you…the hell with it, Lauren, will you marry me?'

'Let's see, I have to cope with a grumpy old patient in recovery, a pregnant sister-in-law with a kid that'll make the place ring with its cries, a dodgy estate on its way to financial recovery and husband who'll be rocketing around the country arranging horse displays.' His face fell, then she stepped forward and he instinctively folded her into his muscular arms, pulling in her into his strong body, his strength and musky scent enveloping her. She tilted her chin upwards, tears of joy sparkling in her eyes, 'the answer is yes.'

They celebrated with a bottle of champagne that Nathan had thoughtfully stored in the boot of his car along with a hamper of fine foods. He wouldn't be able to drive, but as they later settled into a deep embrace, they knew neither of them would be going anywhere for quite a while.

www.ingramcontent.com/pod-product-compliance
Lightning Source LLC
Chambersburg PA
CBHW051422170626
46809CB00006B/2283